KU-351-056

The House of the Deer

At very short notice Gerald Burleigh Brown is
asked to take a deer stalking holiday in place of
his brother-in-law, who has to deal with a security
threat to the shipyard which they manage. The
old hunting lodge where Gerald stays is high up
in the hills, miles from the nearest village and
surrounded by the forest with its high rocky hills,
sparkling silver burns and grassy valleys where the
red deer feed—an enchanting background to an
unusual and exciting chain of events. Apart from
getting to know the other men and attractive girls
in the house party, Gerald gradually begins to
understand and make friends with the local
inhabitants. His days are spent stalking the
'hummel', a huge hornless stag which proves
particularly elusive. Then suddenly an outburst of
violence changes the whole nature of his
holiday. In trying to protect the girl he has grown
to love Gerald runs into considerable personal
danger as the novel moves to its climax.

By the same author

Mrs. Tim
Mrs. Tim Carries On
Mrs. Tim Gets a Job
Mrs. Tim Flies Home
Celia's House
Listening Valley
The English Air
Spring Magic
Miss Bun the Baker's Daughter
Rochester's Wife
Miss Buncle's Book
Miss Buncle Married
The Two Mrs. Abbotts
The Four Graces
Green Money
Vittoria Cottage
Music in the Hills
Winter and Rough Weather
Kate Hardy
Young Mrs. Savage
Five Windows

Charlotte Fairlie
Amberwell
Summerhills
The Tall Stranger
Anna and Her Daughters
Still Glides the Stream
The Musgraves
Bel Lamington
Fletcher's End
The Blue Sapphire
Katherine Wentworth
Katherine's Marriage
Smouldering Fire
The House on the Cliff
Rosabelle Shaw
Sarah Morris Remembers
Sarah's Cottage
Crooked Adam
Gerald and Elizabeth
The Young Clementina

D. E. Stevenson

The House of the Deer

Collins
St James's Place, London 1970

ISBN 0 00 221321 4
© Dorothy Emily Peploe, 1970
Printed in Great Britain
Collins Clear-Type Press
London and Glasgow

In memory of D.W.M.
who killed the Hornless Stag

Contents

I Which introduces Sir Walter MacCallum and his family

Gerald Burleigh Brown had received an invitation to dine at Birkhill. He was *persona grata* at Birkhill, and dined there at least once a week, but this was 'a special occasion' for it was Alastair MacCallum's ninth birthday and Alastair was being allowed to sit up for dinner as a birthday treat.

As Gerald turned in at the gate and drove up to the front door he remembered his first visit to Birkhill. It was almost a year ago now and he had approached the house with very different feelings for having arrived in Glasgow only that afternoon he was a stranger in a strange land. It seemed a good deal more than a year ago – so much had happened in the interval – but all the same he remembered every detail clearly. At that time Sir Walter MacCallum was a widower; his mother lived with him and kept house for him and his small son.

They had dined well – Sir Walter appreciated good food – and when they had finished dinner Gerald had been taken to Sir Walter's study to talk business. He had been informed that his host's 'greatest ambition in life' was to become his brother-in-law and had been asked if he had any objections to offer.

Gerald had no objections: he liked Sir Walter immensely and felt sure he was the right man for Bess. He was older than Bess, (but not more than forty) he was good-looking and friendly and kind. He was the owner of MacCallum's Ship-Building Yard which was an exceedingly well-run and efficient concern and, although he was a Great Man in his own line of business, there was 'no nonsense' about him.

Who could have objected to a brother-in-law so admirable in every way?

Unfortunately there was an obstacle to the marriage, which at the time had seemed insurmountable, but when this had been surmounted (chiefly by Gerald's efforts) Walter and Bess had been married; Gerald had been given a responsible post in MacCallum's Ship-Building Yard; old Lady MacCallum had moved to Bournemouth and Bess reigned in her stead.

Gerald parked his car in the drive and walked in; there was no need to ring the bell and disturb Frost . . . but Frost had heard the car and appeared from the back premises to welcome him and to take his hat.

'Hullo, Frost!' said Gerald. 'It's a lovely evening, isn't it?'

Frost agreed and added that Sir Walter had been delayed but would be ready in ten minutes. Then he opened the drawing-room door and Gerald went in and sat down in a comfortable chair.

The room looked different now, for old Lady MacCallum had taken her goods and chattels to Bournemouth in three enormous vans and Bess had brought her own furniture from her flat in London. It was a great improvement: the well-shaped room seemed larger without the clutter of small tables and uncomfortable little chairs. It was restful and spacious.

Gerald had been sitting in the drawing-room for not more than two minutes when a gruff voice announced fiercely:

'Fee, fie, fo, fum,
'I smell the blood of an Englishman!
'Be he alive, or be he dead,
'I'll grrrind his bones to make my brrread.'

'Help!' shouted Gerald, leaping from his chair and seizing the poker.

A small pink face rose up from behind a big sofa, it was

grinning from ear to ear. 'Were you frightened, Uncle Gerald?' demanded the imp.

'Terrified!'

'I thought you would be. You didn't know I was there, did you?'

'No, I thought you would be in bed. Why aren't you in bed?'

'Because it's my birthday, of course. You knew it was my birthday, didn't you? . . . and I expect that parcel is for me,' declared Alastair, emerging from his hiding-place. He was followed by a smaller boy with bright red hair and bony knees, who stood and looked at Gerald somewhat sheepishly.

'That's Thom Two,' said Alastair. 'I've told you about him, haven't I, Uncle Gerald?' He gave his friend a push and added, 'Go on, you ass! Say how d'you do.'

'Thom Two' walked forward and he and Gerald shook hands solemnly.

Alastair had now seized the parcel and was tearing the paper with small strong hands. Thom Two knelt down on the floor beside him and whispered, 'But, MacCallum, you haven't said "Thank you".'

'I know,' replied 'MacCallum'. 'I'm just waiting to see what it is. If it's a shunting engine for my electric train it will need five times more "thank yous" than if it's a box of chocolates – or anything else. Come on, you can help me to open it.'

Two small pairs of hands made short work of the brown paper wrappings . . . and as it happened to be a shunting engine for an electric train suitable thanks were rendered to the donor:

'Thank you, thank you, thank you, thank you, thank you!' said Alastair, seizing his uncle's hand and shaking it enthusiastically. 'It's absolutely super. I don't know how you guessed I wanted a shunting engine!'

There was no mystery about it – not really – for Gerald was a skilled electrical engineer and when anything went wrong with the electric train system he was called in to 'sort it'. He enjoyed this job for he was very fond of Alastair and the electric trains were the best that money could buy; the rails were laid out all over the floor in one of the spare bedrooms with stations and bridges and level-crossings and tunnels and signal boxes in the appropriate places . . . and, having discovered that Walter's present to his son was a goods station with extensive sidings, Gerald had 'guessed' that a shunting engine would be required.

The shunting engine had been examined and admired and the boys were gathering up the torn paper from the drawing-room floor when the door opened and Bess came in, followed by Walter.

Bess rushed at the guest and hugged him. 'Darling Flick! I haven't seen you for ages!' she exclaimed. 'What have you been doing?'

'Working, of course,' replied Gerald.

'You haven't seen him for four days – not since Tuesday evening,' said Walter laughing.

'Oh, it's all very well for you! You see him every day,' retorted Bess, joining in the laughter. 'You saw him this morning, I suppose. You're overworking Flick – that's what you're doing! The poor darling hasn't time to come and see his sister.'

'Look, Dad!' cried Alastair, holding up his newly-acquired treasure. 'Look what Uncle Gerald has given me! It's a shunting engine – exactly what I wanted. Isn't it absolutely super?'

The party was now complete so the five members of it went into the dining-room and sat down to their meal. The two younger members ate in complete silence, their elders chatted.

'Have you seen an evening paper, Walter?' Gerald inquired. 'I brought you one in case you hadn't. There's a good deal more about the robbery at Keble and Kidd's Yard. The police have caught two of the gang – the others got away.'

'I'd like to see the paper afterwards,' said Walter nodding.

Alastair stopped eating and announced, 'Everybody at school was talking about it this morning. Mr Merryman said they stole all the men's wages for a whole week – it was thousands of pounds.'

'How awful!' Bess exclaimed. 'Don't they have men to guard the money? I mean there have been so many robberies lately. They should have been more careful, shouldn't they, Walter?'

'Their security measures were inadequate,' agreed Walter.

'Dad, how do we guard the money?' inquired his son.

'We take adequate precautions.'

'What sort of precautions?'

'Our security measures are secret.'

'Does Uncle Gerald know about them?'

'I, alone, am responsible for our security measures,' replied Sir Walter firmly.

'But I want to know,' explained Alastair. 'Everybody at school wants to know so I said I would ask you.'

'You have asked me and I have given you my reply: the security measures at MacCallum's are secret.'

'But Dad, you always tell me things about the yard! I'll promise faithfully not to tell anybody if you like. I'll just say it's a secret, so I can't tell them about it.'

'You will not,' said Sir Walter sternly. 'If anybody asks you about the security measures at MacCallum's you will say that you know nothing about them. You will say that your father refused to answer your questions and that he, alone, is responsible for the safety of the yard.'

Alastair gazed at him in silence.

'Do you hear what I say, Alastair?' shouted Sir Walter, thumping on the table with his fist.

Alastair nodded. He couldn't speak. His lips were trembling and his eyes were full of tears.

Gerald was amazed: he had never before known Walter speak and act intemperately. It was completely out of character. He was a gentle man – especially gentle in his dealings with his son – no wonder the boy was alarmed! The other boy was upset too, Gerald noticed.

Fortunately dinner was over so the boys escaped. They ran upstairs to play with the trains and the adults went into the drawing-room for coffee.

'Walter, you frightened them!' exclaimed Bess.

'I meant to frighten them,' replied Walter. He picked up the evening paper which Gerald had brought and sat down to read it.

It was such a lovely evening that Bess and Gerald opened the french windows and went out into the garden. The light was fading but it was quite mild. They were happy to be together – Bess put her hand through Gerald's arm.

At last she said, 'He's dreadfully upset, Flick. It's the robbery, of course. I suppose it might have happened at MacCallum's?'

'No, it couldn't.'

'What do you mean?'

'Our security measures are adequate,' replied Gerald smiling down at her.

'Do you mean you know about them?'

'Yes.'

'But he said you didn't!'

'He didn't say that. What he said was: "I, alone, am responsible for our security measures" – and of course it's true. He's responsible for them; I'm merely the stooge who obeys his orders.'

'I thought you were helping with the electrical equipment of the new German ship.'

'I was.'

'You're chatty tonight, aren't you?'

Gerald smiled. 'My job has been changed. Walter asked me to be his "private secretary".'

'Is it a "rise"?'

'I'm getting more money – if that's what you mean.' (It didn't matter telling her that much.)

'But you don't like it?'

'Some of it is very interesting indeed, but some of the work is – is rather unpleasant.'

'The security measures,' said Bess, who was no fool.

Gerald was silent.

'Oh well, if you won't tell me you won't tell me,' said Bess. 'But why did you agree to do it?'

'Because Walter asked me. When Walter gave me a job in MacCallum's Yard I made up my mind that I would do anything for him (I made up my mind that I would be happy to clean his shoes) and my feelings haven't altered. I'm very fond of your husband, Bess.'

'I know. That's what makes everything perfect.'

'Are you happy?'

'Yes,' she replied. 'Walter and I love each other more and more. He's so considerate, so gentle! (I never saw him behave as he did tonight.) I should be a funny kind of person if I were not happy with Walter . . . and Alastair is a pet.'

'You don't miss all the fun and excitement?'

'No.'

'I just wondered,' explained Gerald.

The fun and excitement to which he referred was Bess's success on the London stage. As Elizabeth Burleigh she had played the principal part in *The Girl from Venus*; she had been admired and fêted, idolised by her fans. Hundreds of people had stood for hours in the rain to see

her. Her name had been blazoned in neon light over the
portico of the theatre; her portrait had appeared in all
the picture-papers. She had been showered with bouquets,
half-buried in fan mail, pursued by men who were anxious
to marry her – or to take her to Paris for a holiday!

Then, at the height of her fame, Bess had married Walter
MacCallum and bowed herself out.

'It *was* fun,' said Bess thoughtfully. 'But I was beginning
to get a bit tired of the fuss. I was beginning to feel I wasn't
real. I was acting all the time. I'm glad I've done it (and
made a success of it) but I'm not sorry it's over. I'm Walter's
wife now and I think I'm making a success of my life as a
real live woman.'

'I'm sure you are. You're a success with Alastair too.'

'I'm hoping to be a success with Margaret.'

'Margaret?' asked Gerald.

'Margaret is coming. Oh, not for months, but when she
does arrive I want you to be her godfather. You will, won't
you?'

'Of course I will!' agreed Gerald. He kissed Bess and
added, 'I'm so glad, darling! Glad about Margaret, I mean.
Take care of yourself, won't you?'

'I'll take care of myself and Margaret,' replied Bess,
smiling happily.

(Gerald was not surprised that Bess had chosen the name.
In all the wonderful stories Bess had told him when they
were children the heroine had been 'Margaret'.)

They walked on round the rose-garden and sat down
together on a teak seat. It was quite dark now but there was
a silvery glow in the sky which heralded the rising moon.

'Supposing it isn't Margaret?' inquired Gerald, after a
long silence.

'If it isn't Margaret it will be Gerald. He will be just as
dear and precious of course. Gerald MacCallum sounds
nice, doesn't it?'

Gerald didn't agree. He said tactfully, 'It's very sweet of you, Bess, but I think it ought to be Donald or Malcolm or Iain, or, perhaps, Colin? Colin was Walter's father's name, wasn't it? What does Walter think about it? I expect Walter is tremendously pleased—'

'I haven't told Walter,' interrupted Bess.

'You haven't told Walter? But Bess—'

'Oh, I shall, of course! But not until after his holiday. He has arranged to go and stay with some friends in the north of Scotland for the stalking. It will be good for him to have a complete break and he wouldn't go if I told him. See?'

'Stalking?' asked Gerald in surprise. It sounded an unlikely sort of holiday for Walter MacCallum.

'Yes. His friends have a deer forest where they shoot stags.'

'How can you shoot stags in a forest?'

Bess was chuckling. 'Oh, Flick, how ignorant you are! There are no trees in a deer forest. It consists of moors and rocks and burns and bogs and bens.'

'Why do you call it a forest?'

'Because that's what it's called,' replied Bess with irrefutable logic. She rose and added, 'I must fly! I must send those children to bed. You had better have a chat with Walter before you go.'

2 In which various matters are discussed and planned

Walter was in his study. He looked up from a letter he was writing and smiled. 'Well, what have you and Bess been plotting? I saw you in the rose-garden talking very seriously indeed.'

'Bess was telling me about your plans for a holiday. What have you been doing?'

'I've been busy,' replied Walter, laying down his pen. 'You'll be glad to hear I've made my peace with Alastair and the tom-tit. I was shown the shunting engine at work, it did its stuff in a satisfactory manner. Then I sent Alastair to have his bath and took the tom-tit home to its nest. I had a few words with its parent, who resembles his chick closely: small and bony with red hair and bright brown eyes. An intelligent bird! I returned home, tucked Alastair into bed and interviewed a detective who was waiting to see me: a man called Dawson, who is investigating the robbery at K. and K's.'

'You *have* been busy,' said Gerald. 'I've just come to say good night.'

'No. Sit down. I want to speak to you.'

Walter began to fiddle with his paperweight. It was a trick he had when he was arranging his thoughts so his private secretary sat down and waited.

'Dawson was interesting. It's his opinion that the robbery was planned by the man who planned the train-robbery. He admits that he may be wrong but he has cogent reasons.'

'I thought those men had been caught and were under lock and key!'

'Some of the gang were caught but we can't be certain that all of them were. Was the man with the brain apprehended? The man who planned the raid; the man who prepared the ground and made the preparations for it . . . and then watched the results from a safe hiding-place? Yesterday's affair was not on the same grand scale but it was prepared and carried out with the same attention to every detail: the same timing, the same daring, the same method and the same success.'

'That puts rather a different complexion upon it!'

'Yes. The police are up against a ruthless devil—clever, cunning, patient—a genius in his own line of country!'

'Why did Dawson want to see you, Walter? Does he think MacCallum's will be the next objective?'

'He wanted to know what precautions we were taking.'

'Did you tell him?'

'No,' replied Walter. 'I just said I considered our security measures adequate . . . and added that in my opinion the Planner's next objective will be something quite different. All the same we shall continue to practise our security measures; in fact I intend to tighten them up.'

Gerald sighed. In his opinion the security measures at MacCallum's Yard were tight enough already. They were the bane of his life.

There was a short silence. Then Gerald said, 'I don't understand why you thought it necessary to frighten the boys.'

'Don't you?' asked Walter. 'I've told you that the Planner of these raids is a ruthless devil. If by any chance he decided to raid MacCallum's it would be convenient for him to know the details of our security measures; he would go to any lengths to obtain information about them. You and Bess were annoyed with me for frightening the boys but wouldn't it be even more alarming if they were kidnapped and questioned?'

'Kidnapped?'

'Yes. If they went about saying that they knew but had "promised not to tell" they might be believed. Oh, I don't think it's likely but I'm not taking any risks. I spoke to Mr Thom about it (he was in America for three years as an agent for an oil company so he wasn't surprised when he heard what I had to say). He wasn't incredulous, as you seem to be. In fact he took it very seriously. He suggested that the Planner might think we'd feel safe and relax our precautions at MacCallum's – which would give the robbers a better chance of success. I saw what he meant, of course.'

'But you don't agree? You think their next objective will be something quite different?'

Sir Walter nodded. 'Yes. I think the Planner enjoys planning. I think it would bore him to do a repeat per-formance . . . and remember these raids are planned and prepared for months in advance. Suitable men must be found and briefed and inserted in key positions to be ready for the Day. You can't do that all of a sudden.'

'You mean that was done at K. and K.'s?'

'Yes. Dawson said so. The man who drove the van was a member of the gang. He had come to K. and K.'s six months ago with unexceptionable references. They were faked. The man was a bad lot. He had been promised two thousand pounds for driving the van to a certain place where an ambush had been prepared. That was how it was done.'

Gerald was amazed. He said, 'Well, anyhow, it couldn't happen like that at MacCallum's.'

'No, it couldn't. The Planner would have to think of a different scheme.' Sir Walter sighed and added, 'I wish I could see into that man's brain. It would be interesting – to say the least of it.'

Gerald agreed that it would be interesting . . . but, as a matter of fact, he was more interested in what his brother-in-law intended to do to tighten up the security measures at MacCallum's Shipyard.' He put the question as tactfully as he could.

'Don't worry,' replied Sir Walter. 'I intend to cable to Joseph Parker. You won't mind handing over the security measures to him, will you?'

'Joseph Parker?'

'Yes. The chap who tidied up that little muddle at Koolbokie.'

(Gerald couldn't help smiling. 'That little muddle at Koolbokie' seemed to him an understatement of the 'tidying up' which Parker had accomplished.)

'You're pleased, aren't you?' added Sir Walter. 'You don't like snooping? Parker doesn't mind. There's plenty for you to do without the security measures.'

'Parker is welcome to them.'

'Good. You had better wait until he comes and hand over the files. Then you can have your holiday.'

'I thought you wanted me to wait until you had had your holiday? We can't both be away at the same time.'

'My holiday must be put off until later.'

'Why?'

'Various reasons. First and foremost I can't leave Bess. She is pregnant. Oh, she hasn't told me yet. She hasn't told me because she knows I've arranged to go to Ardfalloch and stay with my friends the MacAslans, and she knows I wouldn't go if she told me. She'll wait and tell me her news when I come home. That's her idea.'

Gerald knew this already (but he said nothing of course).

'Anyway I'm not going,' Sir Walter continued. 'Later on, when you come back, Bess and I can have a holiday together. We can go to the Riviera if she feels like it. Then there's this trouble at K. and K.'s. I want to find out all the details

. . . and I want to see Parker when he arrives and tell him what he's to do: he must examine the credentials of every man who has come to MacCallum's during the last year – examine them very carefully indeed.'

'That includes me, of course,' said Gerald.

'So it does!' exclaimed Sir Walter, raising his eyebrows in mock surprise. 'Parker must start with your credentials, Gerald.'

They looked at each other and smiled. They understood each other perfectly and were comfortably aware that this was the case.

'Where do you intend to go for your holiday?' Sir Walter asked.

'I don't know. I might go north for some fishing. Dickenson suggested Uist.'

'You wouldn't consider going to Ardfalloch for the stalking? The MacAslans would be glad to have you.'

'But I don't know anything about it! I don't know your friends – they wouldn't want me! I haven't got a rifle – or anything!'

'Can you handle a rifle?'

'Oh yes! I was in my College team. We shot at Bisley for the Ashburton Shield and didn't do badly . . . but you aren't serious, are you?'

'Perfectly serious,' said Sir Walter, smiling. He took up a letter which was lying on his table and added, 'I was just going to answer this. It's from young MacAslan. His name is Gregor but he likes people to call him Mac. His father is MacAslan, the chief of his clan. He owns a large property in the Highlands.'

'A deer forest,' said Gerald nodding.

'Yes, a deer forest, grouse-moors, a sea loch with an island in the middle of it, pine woods, hills with sheep, and a few stony fields of hay, oats, turnips and potatoes. Last but not least, a comfortable house on the shores of the loch.'

'A wealthy landowner!'

'No, a poor landowner. You don't make money on that sort of property unless you can let it to a wealthy sportsman – and there aren't many of that kind going about nowadays. He *does* let occasionally, when he has to, but he loves Ardfalloch so he hates letting it to strangers.'

'That's natural, isn't it?'

'The property is a big responsibility,' continued Sir Walter. 'It has to be looked after if you don't want it to deteriorate. MacAslan can't afford a large staff of keepers and gillies so he and Mac do a lot themselves. I had promised to go up for ten days or a fortnight to help them to cull the deer. I thought perhaps you might like to go instead of me.'

'How do you cull deer?'

'You shoot them.'

'Shoot them?' echoed Gerald in horrified tones.

Sir Walter laughed. 'A certain number of deer must be killed every year to prevent the herd from increasing.'

'But why don't they want their herd to increase?' asked Gerald in bewilderment.

'Because there's only a limited supply of food for them. I don't know much about other forests but Ardfalloch is high and wild. This means that they must keep their herd down to a certain number, otherwise the beasts would starve before the grass begins to grow.'

'Can't they feed the creatures?'

'It wouldn't be easy,' Sir Walter replied. 'They feed the deer in the New Forest but that's different. In Scotland the forests have no roads or tracks; there are mountains and moors and bogs. As a matter of fact MacAslan said he was going to try feeding the stags this year, as an experiment, so I had a talk with the keeper and told him how to go about it.'

'You told him how to go about it?'

Sir Walter nodded. 'I've always been interested in the red deer. I've bought every book I could find on the subject; he's a noble animal, as wild and free as his native hills.'

'It's all quite new to me,' said Gerald hopelessly. 'I'm sure your friends would rather have someone who knows the ropes.'

'Mac wants a man who would be a congenial companion. Here, you had better read his letter,' replied Sir Walter. 'You needn't read the first page – it's just thanking me for the present I sent him on his birthday – start at page two.'

Mac's writing was large and clear so it was easy to read:

'Dad and I intended to do it ourselves with your help and the two stalkers. Malcolm is very good value – as you know – and we have got another man who is young and keen. Unfortunately Dad has had bronchitis. He is better now but the doctor has forbidden him to do any stalking this year. So Phil has arranged for him to go to Edinburgh and stay with his friends the Maclarens, at Davidson's Mains. It will be much better for him not to be here. Also it will leave Phil free to come to Tigh na Feidh. She has asked Donny Eastwood to come. The two girls will keep each other company and help old Kirsty with the cooking. That is satisfactory – as far as it goes – but I must say I should like a congenial companion, so if you happen to know of anybody who would like to come you might let me have his name. I will write and ask him. Needless to say I am terribly sorry you cannot come yourself but I quite understand. We must hope for better luck next year.

With love and again many thanks for the magnificent present,

Yours ever,

Mac.'

'It's a very nice letter,' said Gerald, handing it back. 'But it doesn't tell me much.'

'I'll tell you anything you want to know.'

'But I don't know what to ask – that's the trouble,' explained Gerald. 'To begin with I thought the name of the place was Ardfalloch?'

'That's the big house. They go up to Tigh na Feidh for the stalking. It's a lodge high up on the edge of the forest. Tigh na Feidh means the House of the Deer – and that's just what it is! It's a queer old place, not what you might call luxurious, but I've always been very happy there. The view is marvellous and I enjoy the absolute peace and quiet.'

'You've been there several times?'

'Often,' replied Sir Walter. 'In fact nearly every year, but not last year because MacAslan let the forest to a syndicate from Manchester. They paid him well and he wanted the money but naturally enough they wanted trophies. They were out for heads with fine antlers so that they could have them mounted and could hang them up on their walls to show their friends what tremendous shikaris they were. See?'

'Not really,' admitted Gerald apologetically.

'It isn't a good thing for a forest to have only the fine stags killed. MacAslan would have preferred a certain proportion of older beasts eliminated; stags that were past their prime and "switches" with deformed antlers. The reason being that a stag in good condition with fine antlers is more likely to sire good calves.'

Gerald understood this. 'It's like race-horses,' he said.

'Yes, but you know where you are with horses. You know their breeding. These creatures are wild and free, they roam over the hills for miles, so the only way to improve the herd is to eliminate those that don't come up to standard.'

'Do they shoot the hinds too?'

'Not until later. You don't want to start killing hinds while they still have their calves running with them. I'll lend you a book about deer,' added Sir Walter. He rose and found a small book with a brown leather cover and handed it to Gerald. 'It's old and shabby but you'll find quite a lot of useful information in it. As far as I know there are no modern books on the subject.'

Gerald accepted the book and put it in his pocket. He said, 'I'll read it, of course, but I doubt if it will help me very much. I mean I wouldn't know how to begin.'

'You would go out with a stalker and do exactly as he tells you. It's difficult for me to explain to you because you haven't seen the place . . . but if you don't mind climbing rocks and scrambling about on steep hillsides you'll get a lot of fun out of stalking without knowing a great deal about it. My guess is that you will find it so interesting that you will soon want to know more.'

Sir Walter paused for a few moments and then added, 'Now I had better tell you about the MacAslan family, hadn't I? We've known them for many years. My father used to go to Ardfalloch for the grouse-shooting but I'm not keen on sitting in a butt and having coveys of birds driven over my head. Stalking is much more sporting. You would like the young MacAslans – I'm sure of that. Mac is a good deal younger than you are. He's twenty-three – and in some ways he's young for his age – but he's a friendly creature, interesting and intelligent, so you would get on with him all right. Phil is his sister; she's a year younger and full of beans. She's good fun. Her friend, Donny Eastwood, is a nice little thing – very quiet and gentle. She lives with her father at Larchester and keeps house for him. He's a professor of economics but he has retired now. He writes books which are so clever that very few people want to read them. It's dull for the girl at home so she enjoys coming up to Ardfalloch for a holiday now and then. She and Phil are fond of each other and have jokes together.'

Gerald nodded. He was not interested in the girls; he had been 'interested' in an American girl – a fair, fairy-like little creature – but she had gone home to America and had married a young man whom she had known all her life. Gerald still thought of Penelope sometimes: thought of her a little regretfully if the truth were told.

'Well, what about it?' asked Sir Walter smiling. 'What shall I say to Mac?'

'You really think I should go?'

'Yes, I do. I'm sure you'd enjoy it.'

'All right, then. Tell him I'm on. I expect I can shoot a deer if somebody leads me to it and puts a rifle into my hands. I'll do my best, anyhow.'

'I'll tell him,' said Sir Walter, laughing. I'll lend you one of my rifles and I'll take you to a rifle-range tomorrow afternoon so that you can have a little practice with it before you go.'

This seemed to end the matter so Gerald thanked him and rose.

'Oh, half a minute, Gerald!' Sir Walter exclaimed. 'You had better cable to Joseph Parker; he's at Wellington in New Zealand; you'll find the address in my files.'

'What shall I say?' asked the private secretary, producing a notebook.

'Say "Come earliest possible" and sign it "Shipman". Send it yourself, tomorrow morning.'

The private secretary repeated his orders, said good night and went home.

3 In which an inoffensive gentleman airs his views

When Gerald arrived at the office on Wednesday morning the door-keeper greeted him as usual and informed him that a man had called to see him.

'Who is he, Ballantyne?' asked Gerald.

'He refused to give his name, just said he wanted to see Mr Burleigh Brown. I told him that he ought to have made an appointment but he replied that he would wait.'

Gerald hesitated. Now that he was Sir Walter's private secretary he had a great many callers and he had found that some of them wasted his time.

'He's respectable-looking. Very inoffensive,' said Ballantyne. 'He's small and thin and neatly dressed.'

'Inoffensive?' asked Gerald. 'Hasn't got a gun in his pocket? Well, if you're sure of that you can send him up to my office in about twenty minutes.'

'I'll frisk him,' said Ballantyne, laughing.

Gerald had been given a small room as his private office; there was a big solid table in it and several wooden chairs: what with these and the filing cabinets there was scarcely space to move . . . but it was his very own and he appreciated his privacy. As he hung up his hat on a peg behind the door he remembered his first meeting with Ballantyne. He had been somewhat in awe of the man's imposing appearance and manner. It was different now for they were friends and could have little jokes. Most of the people in MacCallum's appreciated a joke and none of them presumed upon an informal approach. In this respect – as in many others – they were quite different from the men who had worked in the diamond mine in South Africa.

There was a pile of letters on Gerald's table, so he got down to work without delay. It saved time if he could get the morning mail opened and sorted before the arrival of Sir Walter . . . and time was important. Gerald was in a constant state of surprise at the amount of work his brother-in-law got through in a day. Walter's brain was crystal clear and extraordinarily retentive. It was seldom that he had to be reminded of a name or an engagement and he knew all the men in the Shipyard by headmark; he never cluttered up his mind with useless details but grasped essentials and made decisions quickly. The more Gerald saw of the man the more he admired him.

Gerald was half-way through his morning task when there was a knock on his door and Ballantyne ushered in the visitor:

'Gentleman to see you, Mr Burleigh Brown,' said Ballantyne.

The visitor was a complete stranger but he was exactly as Ballantyne had said: very respectable-looking, neat and tidy, small and thin and inoffensive. He waited until Ballantyne had gone and then put a paper on the table in front of Gerald and said,

'There's my calling-card, Mr Burleigh Brown.'

The 'calling-card' was the cable that Gerald had despatched on Saturday morning to Joseph Parker in Wellington.

Gerald sprang up and shook hands with his visitor. 'Good heavens, you haven't wasted time!' he exclaimed.

' "Earliest possible",' quoted Parker.

'I know, but still . . .'

'And signed "Shipman",' Parker added, sitting down on the chair Gerald had drawn up to the table for him.

'It's a code-word, is it?'

'Not exactly. I'll tell you about it sometime. We had better get to business first, hadn't we? I've just arrived and came straight to the office.'

'Sir Walter has gone to the Tail of the Bank this morning so I had better put you in the picture. I'm his private secretary and I'm in charge of the security measures – but I'm to hand over to you. Have you had breakfast? Would you like a cup of coffee and a sandwich?'

Parker replied that he had had a cup of tea on the plane but he could do with something more substantial so Gerald rang his bell and ordered the food. (There were advantages in his position as secretary to a Great Man.) A message-boy was despatched to a nearby restaurant with the order; meanwhile the secret file was produced and opened.

'I guessed it was the Keble and Kidd robbery,' said Parker. 'I read about it, of course. The gang attacked the van on the way from the Bank to the Yard. That's right, isn't it?'

Gerald nodded. 'I'll tell you what we're doing. Then you can study the files.'

The coffee and sandwiches had arrived by this time so Parker ate his meal and listened.

First of all there was 'Operation Pie' which was Sir Walter's own invention: a bullet-proof van had been painted to resemble the fleet of vans which belonged to a large and flourishing Glasgow bakery, the chairman of which was a personal friend of Sir Walter's. (He had laughed inordinately when the scheme had been proposed to him and had suggested several improvements.) Once a week the van was driven to a garage which was next door to the Bank – ostensibly for servicing. All the vans were serviced at the same garage – MacBride's (MacBride was the brother-in-law of Dickenson, a foreman at MacCallum's and completely trustworthy; he had been at MacCallum's for fifteen years.) The van was serviced on a different day each week and at a different hour. The money for the men's wages was packed in cardboard cartons, labelled 'pies' or 'cakes' or 'sausages'. These were carried out of a side door and packed into the van, which already contained trays of real pies and buns and chunks of fruitcake. The van was then driven to the Shipyard. On arrival it drove to the canteen to unload the food. The cardboard cartons were unloaded at the same time and carried down a flight of stone steps to a cellar below the canteen which had been built during the war as an air-raid shelter. They were stacked in a corner of the cellar until required.

'Here's the file about "Operation Pie",' added Gerald, passing it over. 'It contains the names of the men who are in the know. They've all been at MacCallum's for at least six years. If you can suggest any alteration in the scheme you can tell Sir Walter. I'm thankful to get rid of it.'

'It's very ingenious,' was Parker's comment.

The other security measures were more conventional and consisted of electric wires in certain places (which were hidden below the ground and set off alarm bells when they were trodden upon by an unwary foot) and detectives in overalls who patrolled the yard at night with watch-dogs. Gerald did not mind that. His chief objection was the 'snooping'. The credentials of new hands had to be thoroughly examined and men were kept under secret surveillance until it was established that they were neither troublemakers nor spies. He explained all this to Parker and added that he was going away for a holiday and Parker could work here, in his office, until he came back.

'What will you do when you come back?' Parker wanted to know.

'That's up to Sir Walter,' replied Gerald. 'There's plenty of work without the security measures. I'm quite willing to do anything he wants me to do, of course. You know what he did for me. If it hadn't been for Sir Walter that horrible affair at Koolbokie Diamond Mine would never have been cleared up and I should still be going about with a stain on my name.'

Parker knew. It was he who had unravelled the tangled skein at Koolbokie and caught the thief red-handed. He said, 'Yes, but Sir Walter has done a lot more for me. He picked me up out of the gutter when I was eleven years old.'

This was Joseph Parker's story. Gerald heard it that evening when the day's work was done and the two men were relaxing in Gerald's sitting-room in the comfortable little flat which Bess had found for him in a Glasgow suburb.

Joseph was born in a tenement in Maryhill. His father worked in a factory and earned reasonably good pay. His mother made a little extra by cleaning offices so she too was out most of the day and the child was neglected. When Joseph was ten years old his mother died and his father – never very steady – got into bad company and was apprehended by the police for housebreaking. It was decided to send the boy to an institution where he would be looked after and taught a trade but he had a horror of the word 'institution' so he escaped and went off on his own. It was summer-time and for a while he enjoyed his freedom. He wandered about the country, sleeping in barns or under haystacks and by doing little jobs he made a few shillings which he spent on food. It was a different matter when the weather worsened for by that time his clothes were in rags. He drifted back to Glasgow, the only place he knew, but the tenement where he had lived had been pulled down to make room for a garage.

Joseph roved about the streets: cold and hungry and ragged and dirty. When darkness fell he was so dazed and miserable that he staggered off the pavement in front of an approaching car. The car touched his arm and knocked him **over.**

Next moment a strong hand seized him by the collar of his jacket and dragged him out of the gutter and a voice said, 'What d'you think you're doing?'

That was Joseph's first introduction to Walter Mac-Callum. (He was not Sir Walter then, for his father was still alive. He was a young man with a comfortable flat in Glasgow and was on his way home from an evening party.)

A crowd had gathered and a policeman appeared and offered to take the boy to the nearest hospital but Mr MacCallum replied that there was nothing much the matter with the boy. All he needed was a good meal. 'I'll take him home with me and feed him,' said Mr MacCallum.

So Joseph went home with his rescuer. He was put into a hot bath and scrubbed from head to foot; he was wrapped up warmly and sat down at a table near the fire with a good meal before him.

All this time Joseph had not spoken a word (he was completely dumb) but when he had eaten some food his brain began to work and his tongue was loosened. He looked up and said, 'Are you God, mister?'

'No, just a shipman,' replied Walter MacCallum.

Joseph did not remember any more about that evening. He woke the next morning to find himself lying on the sofa in Mister Shipman's sitting-room wrapped in a big brown blanket.

'I stayed with "Mister Shipman" for several days,' continued Joseph. 'He burnt my rags and bought me decent clothes. Then he arranged for me to go and live with Mrs Frost – who had been his mother's cook. She was the mother of Mr Frost who looked after his flat for him. (You know Mr Frost, I expect?)'

'Yes, of course!' said Gerald.

'I was a heathen when I went to live with Mrs Frost, but she was a true Christian, good and kind and motherly. She taught me her own simple faith; she taught me how to behave in a civilised manner. I lived with her for a year and loved her dearly. Then "Mister Shipman" sent me to a boarding-school. I was backward at first but I worked hard and soon made up for lost time. "Mister Shipman" came and saw me quite often and took me out in his car – I knew by then that he was really Mr Walter MacCallum, a partner in his father's ship-building firm, but he was still "Mister Shipman" to me. When I was old enough I went to the Yard, first as a message-boy and later in a special sort of capacity. You see I had had a different life from other boys. I had learnt to be independent; I had learnt to be quick. Sometimes Sir Walter wanted to find out the truth about a man's background – where he went and what sort of friends he had. I was good at that. I was so small and insignificant that nobody noticed me . . .

'That's how it began,' explained Parker. He smiled and continued. 'Sir Walter told me that you don't like "snooping". Well, it isn't a pretty word but I'm not ashamed of snooping. I don't think of it like that. I call it "finding out the truth". I find out the truth about people for Sir Walter. Do you ever read Browning's poems, Mr Burleigh Brown?'

'No.'

'You should,' said Parker. 'There's a lot of meat in them. There's one called "In a Balcony". Parts of it are a bit obscure but one thing is clear. It's this: "Truth is the strong thing: let man's life be true". I like that. If a man's life be true he doesn't need to be afraid of me – or anybody.'

Gerald nodded thoughtfully.

'I'll tell you another thing,' said Parker. 'Nowadays there's too much sympathy for criminals and not enough for their victims. A hundred years ago a man could be hanged for stealing a purse but now the pendulum has swung too far the other way and you can't hang a man for poisoning his grandmother.'

'I'm not really in favour of hanging anybody,' said Gerald in doubtful tones. 'Criminals must be punished, of course, but—'

'Of course!' exclaimed Parker. 'But people tell you that corporal punishment is unchristian. They'll tell you that if a man does wrong you should reason with him gently; you should tell him to be good and not do it again. It's called "binding him over to keep the peace". I'd bind him over, of course, but first I'd give him a darn' good thrashing – just to help him to remember.'

Gerald could not help smiling: there was something very funny about this inoffensive-looking little fellow and the ferocity of his views.

'Oh, you can smile,' nodded Parker. 'But I'm talking from experience. I'm thinking of cases in which I've been involved. I'm thinking of men who deserved thrashing (it would have done them a power of good). I'm thinking of their wrongdoing. I'm thinking of a little girl of seven years old who was waylaid when she was coming home from school. She was taken to a barn and assaulted. Her leg was fractured and she lay there all night in the dark. She didn't die. They took her to hospital and mended her leg but they couldn't mend the damage to her brain. She'll never be the same healthy, happy, friendly little girl she was before. What about it, Mr Burleigh Brown? What punishment would you mete out to the brute who ruined little Nancy?

'Listen,' said Parker, leaning forward in his chair and speaking very earnestly. 'Two thousand years ago there was a Man who found something nasty going on. He found a lot of rogues cheating people in the Temple: they were overcharging and giving the wrong change and making a good thing out of it. Their victims were poor people who were too frightened to complain. I expect the Man stood and watched for a bit – just to make certain. When He had *found out the truth* He took action. He made a whip and thrashed them and upset their tables and sent their ill-gotten gains rolling all over the floor.'

Parker rose and added, 'I'd better be going. I haven't been in bed for three nights so I expect I've been talking too much. I don't often talk like this – in fact I don't remember ever having talked like this before. I'm sorry if I've bored you.'

'You haven't bored me: you've given me a lot to think about. I shan't forget what you've said. Look here, would you like to stay here tonight? I've got a spare room—'

'No, thank you, Mr Burleigh Brown,' interrupted Parker. 'It's very kind of you but it's better if we don't see too much of each other. I don't want people to know I've been talking to Sir Walter's private secretary. I want to keep myself in the background. I can do more that way. I've got your files – I'll study them carefully – and I'll give you my address so you can get in touch with me if necessary. I've taken a room in a Commercial Hotel. A Commercial Hotel is a good place if you want to be inconspicuous; there's a lot of coming and going so nobody notices you.'

Gerald went to the door with him and shook hands.

'By the way,' said Parker. 'You know why I was sent for in a hurry, don't you? He wants me to keep "an unobtrusive eye" on his boy.'

'Alastair! Does he really think Alastair is in danger?'

'Not really,' Parker replied. 'He just wants to take precautions about him and a friend of his. Apparently they go down to the Yard quite often and have the run of the place so it's conceivable that they might know something which would be useful. They're both pretty smart.'

'What do you think?' asked Gerald anxiously.

'I don't think the man who plans these robberies would bother about little boys. He would think they were "just kids" – and beneath his notice. It wouldn't occur to him that they were smart. All the same I intend to be careful. Sir Walter has given me *carte blanche* so I shall get hold of a couple of trustworthy chaps to help me. Those boys will be shadowed all the time – unobtrusively shadowed. See?'

Gerald saw. He said, 'But Parker, what could you do if a man stopped the boys in the street? By the time you had called a policeman—'

'A policeman!' interrupted Parker. 'I wouldn't call a policeman. What would be the good of that? If a man stops those boys in the street I shall put a bullet through his heart without waiting to ask his intentions.'

Parker tapped his pocket significantly, ran down the stairs and disappeared.

For at least ten minutes Gerald stood on the landing wondering what he should do – he weighed several courses of action and rejected them – finally he decided to do nothing and say nothing; the security measures at MacCallum's Shipyard were no longer his business.

4   Which tells of a rendezvous at Ardfalloch Inn

It was a little after twelve o'clock on a fine September day when Gerald arrived in Ardfalloch village and pulled up at the inn. The village was small: just a double row of cottages, a post office, a shop and an inn with M A C T A G G A R T written over the doorway. A stout man with an apron tied round his middle was standing in the doorway and came forward with a welcoming smile.

'Can I leave my car here?' asked Gerald.

'You will be the gentleman who is going to Tigh na Feidh?'

'Yes. Young Mr MacAslan told me to meet him here. Have you got room in your garage for my car?'

'It would be a strange thing if a guest of MacAslan could not be leaving his car at Ardfalloch Inn,' replied Mr MacTaggart.

This seemed satisfactory so Gerald drove into the garage, the doors of which stood open.

The innkeeper followed him and leant against the side of the car. 'This is a very small place,' he said in deprecating tones. 'It must seem very small indeed to a gentleman from Glasgow.'

'It isn't very big,' agreed Gerald.

'The inn belonged to my father so I was born and reared in Ardfalloch,' explained Mr MacTaggart. 'When I was a young man I was not very fond of it so I went to Glasgow and took service in a big hotel. I learned to cook and to wait at table. It was my intention to own a big hotel some day and make a lot of money, but when my father died I came home to Ardfalloch and found a wife.'

'You gave up your ambition,' suggested Gerald.

Mr MacTaggart nodded. 'But there are compensations,' he said grandly. 'In a big town I would be nobody but in Ardfalloch I am Somebody. People come to me for advice. I am Captain of the Fire Brigade – we have smart uniforms and brass helmets – I am President of the Bowling Club. It is better to be a big fish in a wee pond than a very wee fish in a big pond. That is what I am thinking.'

Gerald smiled. 'What does your wife think about it?' he inquired.

'She likes to be a big fish. She is President of the Women's Rural . . . and, though the place is small, we manage none too badly. We have gentlemen for the shooting and the fishing. We are full up during the season. The gentlemen come back year after year and they tell their friends: "You will get good food and a clean bed at MacTaggart's." Och, we manage none too badly. You see there is no competition. There is no other inn . . . except the inn at Balnafin, which is not very clean nor very comfortable. Raddle is not particular about his clients (he will give house-room to anybody) and Mistress Raddle is a very poor cook. The Horseman's Inn would not be nice for a gentleman like you. Not nice at all.'

Gerald was amused at Mr MacTaggart's loquacity. Perhaps the man was a little too pleased with himself but there was something rather nice about him.

'Two years ago,' continued Mr MacTaggart. 'Two years ago Mistress MacTaggart and I decided to launch out. We got a builder all the way from Inverness to make three new bedrooms and another bathroom. The bedrooms have fixed basins with hot and cold water so the gentlemen are willing to pay extra for them. Already we have got back our money and paid off the debt.'

Gerald congratulated him.

'Yes, it was a good spec.,' said Mr MacTaggart proudly. He added, 'But you will not be wanting a bedroom. You will be staying at Tigh na Feidh?'

'Yes.'

'Mac will be meeting you here in the Land-Rover?'

'That's what he said in his letter.'

'That is what he will do. He will be here for lunch and he will be taking you to Tigh na Feidh in the afternoon. How long will you be staying?'

'I'm not sure,' replied Gerald doubtfully. He had received a very polite letter from his prospective host which began, 'Dear Mr Burleigh Brown' and ended, 'Yours sincerely, Gregor MacAslan', but he had sensed a lack of warmth in the letter and, despite Walter's assurance that the young MacAslans would be delighted to have him, he felt certain that they would rather have a guest who knew something about stalking. He had made up his mind that he would stay for a few days and if he found that he was not wanted he would go on somewhere else.

'Och, you will be staying two weeks – or more,' said Mr MacTaggart. 'Miss Phil has ordered plenty of food. It came in the van this morning and I have it ready for Mac when he comes with the Land-Rover. Miss Phil is a very business-like young lady. She would not be ordering all that food if she was not expecting guests.'

Gerald now perceived a pile of sacks and crates and boxes which were stacked in a corner of the garage. 'All that?' he asked in surprise.

'Stalking is hungry work,' explained Mr MacTaggart.

It was nearly half past twelve by this time and Gerald had been told that his prospective host would meet him here at twelve, so he was beginning to wonder if there had been some mistake. Perhaps he should drive on to Tigh na Feidh in his car, taking some of the provisions with him.

Gerald was about to suggest this to Mr MacTaggart when a Land-Rover drove into the yard and out of it jumped a young man with fair hair. He was a very good-looking young man; his figure was slender and graceful; he was as lithe as an athlete in training.

'Hullo, MacTaggart!' he exclaimed. 'Have you got the provisions? Phil said she had sent you a list of what she wanted.'

'It is all here!' replied MacTaggart, hurrying out to meet him. 'The flour and the oatmeal, two sacks of potatoes and two big crates from Inverness. The whisky is here, and the eggs and a side of bacon – everything Miss Phil wanted – and this is the gentleman from Glasgow that you were expecting.'

'Oh, good!' said young MacAslan, coming forward and shaking hands. 'I'm sorry I'm a bit late, Mr Burleigh Brown.'

'Oh, it's quite all right. I was chatting to Mr MacTaggart.'

'These are the things, Mac,' said MacTaggart, pointing to the pile. 'Will I get the lad to pack them for you while you are having lunch?'

'I'll do it myself,' replied young MacAslan. 'Some of the stuff looks a bit too heavy for the lad. Then we can have lunch and go up to the house afterwards.' He turned as he spoke and, seizing an enormous sack of potatoes, swung it on to his back and carried it over to the Land-Rover as easily as if it were stuffed with feathers.

'Can I help you?' asked Gerald.

'Don't bother. It won't take ten minutes,' said young MacAslan, seizing another, even larger, sack and dealing with it in the same way.

Gerald hesitated, wondering what he should do. His help had been refused, somewhat curtly. There were several other sacks but they were all large and looked extremely heavy so he was a little doubtful as to whether he would be able to carry them. He was strong and fit but he was not used

to carrying sacks – and probably there was a knack in this
kind of work. It would be embarrassing if he tried to hoist
the sack on to his back and found himself unable to do so.
The crates looked even more unwieldy!

Another source of embarrassment was the fact that he
did not know how to address young MacAslan. The boy
(he was little more) had addressed him as 'Mr Burleigh
Brown'. Should he call the boy 'Mr MacAslan'? It seemed
silly (and probably it was the wrong thing to do)! Gerald
wished he had asked Walter, but he had taken it for granted
that the boy would be friendly. The boy was polite but he
was not friendly; in fact his manner was distinctly chilly. It
was going to be very difficult, thought Gerald unhappily.

Fortunately he was rescued from his state of indecision
by Mr MacTaggart who suggested that he might like to
wash, adding that lunch was nearly ready and Mrs MacTaggart would be 'put about' if her guests were not prepared to
eat it while it was hot.

'There is nice soup and fresh mackerel from the loch,' said
Mr MacTaggart persuasively.

Gerald allowed himself to be persuaded.

At lunch they talked about the weather. Young MacAslan
said it had been wet yesterday but the glass had gone up so
he hoped it was going to be fine tomorrow. Gerald replied
that it rained a good deal in Glasgow but he was getting
used to it and didn't mind. Young MacAslan said rain was
rather a nuisance but fog was worse. Gerald agreed that
fog was a great deal worse.

When they had said all that they could think of about the
weather there was a short silence.

'I had better tell you,' said young MacAslan at last.
'There's another man coming. We've known him for years so
when he wrote and asked if we could have him we couldn't
refuse. He lives with his mother in Glasgow and goes about

a good deal so perhaps you know him. His name is Oliver Stoddart.'

'I've never met him,' Gerald replied. 'As a matter of fact my job keeps me pretty busy so I haven't got to know many people in Glasgow – but don't worry, it doesn't matter a bit.'

'What do you mean?'

'I mean if you haven't room for me I can easily—'

'Oh, it isn't that! We've got plenty of room for you both. I just want to explain about Oliver. He's in some sort of business in Glasgow but he doesn't seem to have to do much work. He lives with his mother (I told you that) and he has lots of money so he goes about all over the place, staying with friends and shooting and fishing. Last year he went to New Zealand and the year before to Norway – there's very good fishing in Norway. He asked me to go with him, but I couldn't of course. I mean I couldn't ask Dad for the money and anyhow there's plenty to do here . . .'

Gerald listened to all this and wondered what was coming.

'Oliver is a good shot. He has been here several times and enjoys stalking. He says in his letter that he wants some good heads and he's willing to pay for his sport. I asked my father about it and he said the money would be useful . . . so there you are.'

'Where am I?' asked Gerald, smiling.

'Where are you? Oh, I see what you mean! I'm not very good at explaining things. The fact is we didn't intend to shoot good stags this year and Sir Walter said you didn't mind.'

'I don't mind in the least, but all the same I'm quite willing to pay the same as your friend.'

'You can't do that.'

'Why not?'

'It wouldn't be fair.'

'Look here, let's get this straight. Sir Walter explained about what happened last year when you let the deer forest to a syndicate and he told me that this year you wanted the less good animals shot. Well, that suits me. I'll shoot the ones you tell me to shoot – if I can. I want to learn about stalking. I want the fun of the sport and I'm quite prepared to pay—'

'You can't do that,' repeated Mac. He added, 'If you pay the same as Oliver you must have the same sport. It wouldn't be right to take your money and not give you the chance of killing a good stag. It wouldn't be fair.'

'But I don't want to kill a good stag! I'd rather not.'

'You'd rather not?'

'I'd like to look at him,' Gerald explained. 'I'd like to see him standing on his own hills in all his glory – and let him go. I'd rather shoot a stag with crooked horns. That's what you want, isn't it?'

'That's what we intended to do this year. That's what we *would* have done if my father had been fit and Sir Walter hadn't been tied up in Glasgow.'

'I've come instead of Sir Walter,' Gerald pointed out.

'I know . . . and it sounded all right until Oliver wrote and said he wanted to come.'

'It's perfectly all right. The fact that your friend is coming doesn't change the arrangement as far as I'm concerned.'

'It does,' objected Mac. 'It wouldn't be fair to take your money—'

'You've said that before,' Gerald interrupted. 'I can only repeat that I've come instead of Sir Walter.'

'We're going round in circles,' said Mac. He thought for a few moments and then added, 'All right, we'll compromise. You will shoot switches and beasts that are past their prime, but I won't take a penny from you. That's flat.'

It was not a compromise but Gerald saw that he was adamant and was obliged to agree. 'There's just one more thing I want to say,' declared Gerald. 'I've come to help you, so if you find I'm useless you'll tell me quite honestly—'

'Oh, you'll be useful! It's like this, you see. We can't afford a big staff of keepers and stalkers so we do a lot ourselves. Phil is almost as good as a boy,' added Phil's brother in patronising tones.

'How do you mean?' inquired the guest.

'She's a good shot with a gun and she doesn't mind killing foxes – they're very troublesome, of course – but stalking is a man's sport.'

'I'm pretty fit,' Gerald assured him. 'My job at Mac-Callum's isn't strenuous physically, but it isn't sedentary either. There's a good deal of running about the Yard – it's an enormous place, you know – and I take as much exercise as I can. I play squash in the evenings when I have time.'

'What is your job – exactly?'

'I'm dog's-body to Sir Walter,' replied Sir Walter's private secretary.

Mac looked at his guest critically and decided that he looked pretty fit, which was satisfactory.

'I've never done any stalking,' Gerald added. 'I expect you've realised that I know nothing about it.'

Mac had. He said rather anxiously, 'Sir Walter said you could shoot?'

'I've shot lions,' admitted Gerald. 'But that's different, of course.'

Mac began to laugh . . . and couldn't stop. He laughed and laughed and laughed. It was the laughter of a boy and so infectious that Gerald laughed too.

'But I don't know why we're laughing,' said Gerald at last.

'Don't you?' gasped the boy, wiping his streaming eyes. 'Oh lord! Just wait till I tell Phil!'

'I don't understand—'

'Well, quite honestly,' gasped Mac. 'Quite honestly Phil

and I – had a feeling – that you were a bit of a milksop. I don't know – why, exactly—'

'It wasn't for sport,' said Gerald, trying to explain. 'I had to kill them because they were such a nuisance—'

'Oh don't!' cried Mac in agonised tones. 'Don't say another word or you'll start me off again . . . and I'm sore all over.'

Obediently Gerald was silent and, after a few more chuckles, Mac drank some water and calmed down.

The laughter had cleared the air so things were more comfortable. Gerald felt the warmth in the atmosphere and responded to it by suggesting Christian names.

'I hoped you'd say that,' agreed Mac, smiling cheerfully. 'You're older than I am, of course, but you can't stalk all day with a man and not be friends.'

'Mr MacTaggart called you Mac.'

'They all do; it's a compliment really – a sort of title. My father is MacAslan and I'm Mac. That reminds me we had better fetch the letters at the post office before setting out to the forest. I'm expecting one from my father. You could nip along and get them, couldn't you? I'll just see what sort of a hash MacTaggart's lad has made of packing the provisions. Mrs MacTaggart wouldn't let me finish the job.'

Gerald 'nipped along' and asked for the letters – there was a sheaf of mail waiting – and a few minutes later he and Mac were on their way to Tigh na Feidh.

5 Tells of Gerald's arrival at the House of the Deer

Gerald had wondered why he could not have driven to his destination in his own car. The reason became obvious: only a vehicle with a four-wheel drive could have ascended the rutty track. There was a gate leading off the road, then came a hump-backed bridge over a rocky stream; after that the track wound its way up the hill with hair-pin bends, which necessitated backing. After that they came to a cut in the hills with towering cliffs on either side. Here the road narrowed and wound its way between huge boulders of igneous rock.

'This is called the Black Pass,' said Mac. 'It isn't really as perilous as it looks – and I'm used to it, of course.' As a matter of fact he was quite pleased with his passenger for showing no signs of fear. Most people blenched and clutched the sides of the vehicle. Some had been known to scream. This passenger merely inquired, 'What happens if you meet another car?'

'You don't often. If you do one or other of you has to back till you get to a passing place . . . like that, for instance,' replied Mac, pointing to a small quarry which looked to Gerald like a slimy bog.

'Phil said I had better warn you that there are no luxuries at Tigh na Feidh,' he continued. 'There's no electricity – just lamps – and no telephone. The roof leaks a bit here and there, but only in very heavy rain. We ought to have it seen to, of course, but we only use the house for the stalking so it doesn't seem worth while. Malcolm lives here all the year round with his mother but they don't mind.'

'Who is Malcolm?'

'He's the head stalker. He's been with us for years and years – ever since I can remember. If you want to know anything about deer you can ask Malcolm. He'll talk about deer for hours. My father is very knowledgeable too, but he's not here this year.'

'He has been ill, hasn't he?'

'He had rather a bad go of bronchitis. He's better now, thank goodness! But the doctor said it would be madness for him to do any stalking. That's why Phil made him go to Edinburgh.' Mac sighed and added, 'It's awfully queer to be living at Tigh na Feidh without Dad.'

By this time they had emerged from the Pass into the sunlight. Mac drew up and said, 'There it is, Gerald. That's the House of the Deer. It's a queer old place, isn't it? Long ago it was a Look-Out Tower (it has a wonderfully wide view in all directions) but it was neglected until it became almost ruinous. My great-great-grandfather renovated it and built on to it so that it could be used for stalking. He got the local builder and they built on rooms as and when they were needed for his family and his friends and made steps up to them and little passages – and added a few turrets just for fun – so Tigh na Feidh is a higgledy-piggledy mess. It's an architect's nightmare! All the same there's something rather attractive about it – at least Phil and I think so. We're fond of it,' added Mac apologetically.

Gerald looked at the old house with interest. It was on the side of a hill near a burn and was built of rough grey stone. The windows were on different levels and were of different sizes and shapes: some were large and square, others were small and oblong. Those facing west were built into a kind of bow, like half a tower. Above that the half tower became a whole tower with windows facing in three directions. The roof, which was made of slate, was steep and uneven, gables jutted out at all angles and twisted chimneys sprouted in unexpected places. The pepper-pot turrets which had been added 'just for fun' gave the place a rakish appearance.

'I've never seen anything like it!' Gerald exclaimed.

'No, and you never will,' declared Mac, smiling.

The House of the Deer was unique inside as well as outside. There was one large room which ran through the centre of the house on the ground floor and had windows facing east and west. It was used as a sitting-room at one end and as a dining-room at the other.

This was the old part of the house, as could be seen from the thickness of the walls. The windows were set in deep embrasures which were filled with cushioned window seats. Half-way down one side of the room there was a huge stone fire-place with a wrought iron grate for burning logs. The furniture consisted of large chairs upholstered in brown leather (which probably had been new in Victorian times) and large bookcases containing books about fishing and shooting and the habits of deer. There was a work-basket, bulging with grey woollen stockings, on one chair and a pile of papers on another . . .

Mac seized the work-basket and chucked it on to the floor. 'Sit down, Gerald,' he said hospitably. 'This place isn't very tidy, I'm afraid, but we use it for everything. Old Kirsty does her best to keep it tidy but Phil and I aren't tidy people so we don't mind . . . and, anyhow, it isn't a lady's drawing-room. It's just a place to relax when you come in from the hill, dirty and tired and cold.'

He added, 'We have a meal at six-thirty when we're here: fish and chips or sausages – or venison, of course – so there's plenty of time for a walk up the burn if you would like to stretch your legs. I must just look through these letters first in case there's anything important.'

Gerald sat down and waited while his host skimmed

through the letters. He was interested to see that although Mac had admitted to 'untidiness' he was businesslike with the letters. They were divided into several heaps and clipped together. Only one of them was pronounced 'important'.

'I shall have to see Malcolm about this,' Mac explained. 'It's from my father. He says you must be given the chance of killing at least one good stag. We shall probably find Malcolm in the gun-room.'

'But I've told you I don't want—'

'You don't understand,' declared Mac, smiling. 'Mac-Aslan says you're to be given the chance of killing at least one good stag. It's orders. MacAslan's word is Law. Come and talk to Malcolm.'

'Wouldn't you rather talk to Malcolm yourself?'

'You'll be interested to see him; he's a curiosity like Tigh na Feidh. If he likes you he'll show you his map. If he doesn't he won't – and it would be useful for you to see his map. Besides,' added Mac frankly, 'besides, if you're there he'll speak English.'

'Speak English?' echoed Gerald in surprise.

'It wouldn't be polite not to,' explained Mac. Then, seeing that his guest was still bewildered, he elucidated further: 'Dad has the Gaelic and so has Phil, but I've been away so much that I've lost it more or less. First I was at school, then at Edinburgh University and then for the last eighteen months I've been staying in Canada with my half-brother. He's in business – and would have given me a good post in his firm – but I'm needed here. Come on, Gerald!'

The gun-room was a large square apartment on the ground floor. There were stands of guns and rifles and fishing rods; there were antlered heads on the walls; a huge stuffed salmon in a glass case hung over the fire-place. All was in perfect order.

In the middle of the room a man was seated at a table, cleaning a rifle. He was a short thick-set man with brown hair which was so tough and wiry that it stuck out from his head like an ill-trimmed bush. His face was reddish brown, tanned by the weather, and he wore a yellowish brown moustache, rather long and drooping, which gave him a somewhat lugubrious appearance.

'Hullo, Malcolm,' said Mac. 'We've come to talk to you. This is Mr Burleigh Brown, that I told you about. He's a brother-in-law of Sir Walter MacCallum's.'

Malcolm rose and shook hands. Then they all three sat down at the table.

'This is a fine weapon,' said Malcolm, pointing to the rifle he was cleaning. 'It is Sir Walter MacCallum's .303 Express. I was cleaning it two years ago when he was here and I would know it anywhere.'

'Yes, he lent it to me,' Gerald explained.

'Is that so? Sir Walter must think highly of you to lend you this weapon, Mr Burleigh Brown,' declared Malcolm, looking at Gerald with increased respect.

'He's very kind. He took me to a rifle range near Glasgow so that I could have some target practice with it. I cleaned it afterwards very carefully—'

'Och, it is nice and clean,' Malcolm interrupted. 'It is just that I am giving it a wee polish to make sure.'

'Malcolm is never happier than when he's taking rifles to bits,' said Mac, smiling. 'No matter how carefully you clean your rifle he's never satisfied.'

Malcolm smiled too, but did not reply.

'I've never shot deer,' said Gerald. 'I know nothing about stalking but Sir Walter said you would be able to teach me. You'll find me very ignorant, I'm afraid.'

'I will tell you all I can. I have been at Ard na Feidh all my life: first under my father and then as MacAslan's head keeper – but there is still a lot about deer that I do not understand.' Malcolm sighed and added, 'Yes, there is a lot about deer that puzzles me.'

'What about the feeding?' Mac asked. 'MacAslan said you were going to try feeding them this year. Was it a success?'

'It was a good thing. The stags are in fine fettle. By the middle of August there was scarcely a stag in velvet to be seen on the hill. There are some pretty heads, too. I was seeing an eleven-pointer up the glen on Saturday – and there is a fine Royal over towards Ben Ghaoth. Och, he is a fine beast.'

'Tell me about the feeding.'

'It was Sir Walter that suggested it,' explained Malcolm. 'He was telling MacAslan about it so I did it the way he said. I asked Mackenzie for the loan of his tractor – I could not have managed without – and I was putting down the rock salt first. They soon found it! Then I was putting down the potatoes and the beans. I did the feeding early in the morning – like Sir Walter said. One morning when I was going up to the sanctuary there was a score of stags waiting on me. Och, they liked it fine! It was quite tame they were, after a wee while (not minding me at all) but they are as wild as ever now.'

'You really think it was a success?'

'It was indeed,' Malcolm assured him. 'I was not liking the idea of it – you know that, Mac. It seemed a queer thing to be feeding stags, like as if they were cattle, but the food was helping them a lot. I was hearing that they have lost a wheen of stags over at Glen Veigh with the late rut and the long hard winter.'

Mac nodded. He said, 'We shan't be able to do it every year. It costs a lot of money.'

'There will be no need,' Malcolm replied. 'It was the long hard winter that was the trouble. The winters are not always long and hard.' He paused and then added, 'I have never seen so many stags at Ard na Feidh. I am thinking a good many must have come over the river from Glen Veigh. And will you tell me this, Mac: how could they be knowing about the feeding?'

Mac looked at him thoughtfully. 'I wonder,' he said.

'Yes, it is a queer thing. So it is.'

'It isn't what we intended—'

'Och, I know that fine,' interrupted Malcolm. 'But we need not be troubling ourselves. Glen Veigh is an ill-run forest. If Mr Ross is wanting to keep his stags at home he had better feed them (he can well afford it) but it is the grouse-moor he is keen on, not the deer. The young gentlemen are not caring about the forest either. Mackenzie takes them on the hill and they are shooting the first stag they see whether he be a well-grown beast or not. The gentlemen will not content themselves to be taking a switch. It is the good heads they are after. That is not the way to be improving a forest.'

'MacAslan wants us to kill as many switches as possible this year,' said Mac.

'I know that,' agreed Malcolm. 'And that is what we will do. It pleases me to see a switch killed, so it does.'

'Malcolm,' said Mac. 'You remember I told you that Mr Burleigh Brown was quite content to kill switches? Well, I've just had a letter from MacAslan saying that Mr Burleigh Brown must be given the chance of killing at least one good stag, so—'

'MacAslan is always right,' declared Malcolm. 'I have not been happy about it, either. It is not right that a guest should come to Ard na Feidh and be given poor sport. A guest should be given the best a house can offer.'

Gerald was about to object and to explain his views on the subject but a look from Mac silenced him . . . and he remembered that MacAslan's word was Law.

'Maybe you are wanting an easy day tomorrow,' Malcolm was saying.

Mac looked at Gerald inquiringly.

'Just as you like,' replied Gerald. 'I'm perfectly fit for anything. If it's a fine day it would be a pity to waste it.'

'Good!' exclaimed Mac. 'You can meet us in the usual place, can't you, Malcolm?'

The arrangements were made. Then Mac rose and explained that he must deal with the remainder of his letters. 'You don't mind, do you, Gerald?' he said. 'If we're going out early tomorrow I had better get them off my chest. Perhaps Malcolm will tell you about the forest and show you his collection of horns.'

'That is a good plan,' declared Malcolm. 'It would be as well for Mr Burleigh Brown to see the map of the forest before tomorrow morning. Are you interested in maps, Mr Burleigh Brown?'

Gerald was very interested in maps.

'This map is very rough,' declared Malcolm in deprecating tones.

The map was produced from a locked drawer and was laid out carefully on the table.

'Och, it is not a proper map at all!' added Malcolm, looking at his handiwork with feigned disgust. 'It is just a mess – not fit to be shown to a gentleman! I made it for myself, for the fun of it.'

'It seems to be a very good map,' Gerald assured him.

This was true. By looking at the map and following the stalker's explanations Gerald was able to get quite a good idea of the lie of the land.

Ard na Feidh (the Forest of the Deer) was not a large forest. It was about eighteen thousand acres but it was so well distributed that it was able to support more deer per acre than many larger ones. There was high ground and low ground, slopes of grass and heather and little corries where burns ran down to the river . . . and, by the river, was a sheltered holm (or meadow) where the hinds loved to feed. The high ground sloped up to Ben Ghaoth where there were heaps of boulders and screes of loose stones and where snow lay in deep drifts until well on in the spring.

Malcolm knew every yard of the forest, he knew it at all seasons of the year, so he was able to explain his map and to point out the details to his pupil. He also knew a great many of the stags by sight, for he had watched them grow year by year as he went about his work and he had tried to collect their horns and to mark their development. He opened a cupboard in the corner of the room and showed the horns to Gerald.

Fortunately Gerald was aware that stags cast their horns every year and grow new ones. 'How do you find the horns?' he asked.

'It is not easy,' replied Malcolm. 'The hinds like to gnaw them – like a dog gnaws a bone – and I like to collect them when they are in good condition. Here is an interesting thing, Mr Burleigh Brown. Here are three sets of horns which were cast by the same stag three years running. See for yourself! The horns have improved but the number of points remain the same. I am thinking he will improve yet, for he is only nine years old . . . And here is a switch,' he continued, taking up the deformed horn and handing it to Gerald. 'It is an ugly thing, a switch. This beast has grown points this year, but they are not good points at all. If we are seeing him on the hill they will not be saving his life. I do not like to be seeing switches at Ard na Feidh – nor hummels either.'

'What is a hummel, Malcolm?'

'He is a beast without any horns at all – just hard bony knobs where his horns should be – but the queer thing is that he is usually big and heavy. Och, I do not like the look

6 In which a young man is dumbfounded

It was now six o'clock and Gerald had not yet seen his hostess. She had been out when he arrived at Tigh na Feidh but Mac had said that the girls did most of the cooking so probably by this time she would be in the kitchen.

The house was so strangely built – with so many queer little passages – that it was not an easy matter to find the kitchen. Gerald found it by hearing the sound of voices and laughter coming from a room at the end of a corridor. He opened the door and looked in. Yes, here were the two girls, cooking and enjoying a joke.

Gerald had heard quite a lot about Phil MacAslan (Sir Walter had said she was 'full of beans and very good fun'; Mr MacTaggart had said 'Miss Phil is a very businesslike young lady'; her brother had said she was 'almost as good as a boy'). None of these descriptions had interested Gerald, in fact they had 'put him off'. He was struck dumb when he saw her.

She was beautiful – yes, beautiful! She was slender and graceful with dark curls and a smooth creamy complexion, slightly tanned by the sun; her eyes were greeny brown like a mountain burn, sparkling with life.

Phil was standing at the kitchen table, kneading a doughy sort of mess. She looked up and exclaimed, 'Oh, there you are! I'm sorry I was out when you arrived. Donny and I went for a walk. I'm Phil, of course, and this is Donny Eastwood.'

Gerald tried to say, 'I'm Gerald,' but he found that he

couldn't. His lips were so dry that he couldn't utter a word. He stood and gazed at her.

'Mac said you were talking to Malcolm,' said Phil. 'But I expect he was doing most of the talking.'

Gerald moistened his lips and said, 'I'm Gerald, of course.'

'Of course,' said Phil, nodding.

Gerald came forward and held out his hand.

'Mine are all floury,' said Phil. 'I'm making oatcakes for tea, but you can shake hands with Donny. I hope you like oatcakes, Gerald.'

'Yes, I like them very much,' said Gerald.

'Good! We all like them – which means I must make a lot – but I'm so used to making them that I could do it with my eyes shut.' She rolled out the oatcake, cut it into neat triangles and put them on the girdle.

'I'll watch them,' said the other girl, who had not spoken before. 'And I'll grill the trout (shall I?) while you show Mr Burleigh Brown his room. Or would you rather have them fried?'

'Grilled, I think . . . but you had better call him Gerald unless you want him to call you Miss Eastwood.'

Phil rinsed her hands at the sink, took off her apron, flung it on to a chair and turned and smiled at him. 'I'll show you,' she said.

The smile finished Gerald. His heart bounded – and was lost. All in a moment he knew that his heart had gone for ever! She was the most beautiful creature he had ever seen; she was dear and sweet and friendly; she was quite, quite perfect; there was nobody like her in all the world!

Gerald had met girls who attracted him: he had told Bess that he was very fond of Penelope – and it was true. He had told Bess that if Penelope had been the daughter of a grocer (instead of the daughter of an American millionaire and used to every luxury that money could buy) he would have asked her to marry him . . . but he had never felt like this. He had never believed that he could feel like this about a girl.

So this was love! What was more it was love at first sight – a phenomenon which Gerald had always thought impossible! How could you love someone you had never seen before – someone you knew nothing about? Love at first sight was plain silly. It was something you read about in romances. It couldn't happen in real life – but it had happened to him. It had happened because he *did* know her, he knew exactly what she was like. I've been waiting for her all my life, thought Gerald as he followed her upstairs.

Phil led the way along a narrow stone passage; up three steps; round a bend; and down two steps to a little square landing with two doors opening off it. 'That's Mac's room and this is yours,' she explained. 'The roof leaks – you can see the mark on the ceiling – but the bed is comfortable which is the main thing – and the room is fairly warm because it's over the dining-room. The bells don't work, of course, but if you want anything you can hammer on Mac's door, can't you?'

'Yes,' agreed Gerald.

'I wish we could put in fixed basins but the walls are so thick and solid that we can't. There's only one bathroom which is a frightful nuisance. You'll have to fight for your bath, Gerald.'

'Fight for my bath?'

'Yes, you mustn't be polite about it,' explained Phil. 'When you hear the water running away you must lurk in the passage and make a dash for it the moment the door opens. Fortunately we've got a marvellous stove so there's plenty of hot water. That's *absolutely* necessary of course.' She added, 'This room is in the old part of the house. Look how thick the walls are.'

'It's like a fortress!' Gerald exclaimed.

'Perhaps it was – at one time,' said Phil dreamily. 'I wish we knew more about its history. In the old books it's just called "The Look-Out Tower". Daddy thinks that people lived here to keep watch for the approach of enemies and warned the surrounding country by lighting a bonfire . . . but nobody knows *really* because our great-great-grandfather rebuilt it and added on bits and pieces. The view is nice, isn't it?'

They stood at the window together and looked out.

The view was beautiful. There were mountains and rocks, heathery hills and green valleys and little sparkling burns . . . but, to tell the truth, Gerald was so conscious of Phil, standing beside him with her shoulder almost touching his arm, that he was unable to appreciate the view. He felt quite giddy. Then, when she looked up at him, surprised at his silence, he managed to control his feelings.

'It's a good site for a look-out tower,' he said at last.

'Yes, it is,' agreed Phil. 'There's a sort of ladder behind that door in the corner which leads up to one of the funny little turrets. You can see for miles from there. If you've got a telescope you can see deer on the hill. Sometimes, when Daddy and Mac are stalking, I bring a glass and climb the ladder and watch them. It's rather fun. I can see quite a lot of the sport – unless of course they go over the shoulder of Ben Ghaoth – but even then I know what's going on because if the wind is in the right direction I can hear the shot.'

'Phil,' said Gerald. 'I don't want to shoot a stag.'

'I thought you had come for the stalking,' she said in surprise.

'I came because Sir Walter MacCallum said I would be useful. The idea was that I was to help to improve the herd by killing "switches". Malcolm showed me some of the ugly horns he had collected (and explained that the deformities are hereditary) so I wouldn't mind doing that. But now your father has written to Mac saying that I'm to be given the chance of killing at least one good stag. What am I to do?'

'You must do it, of course,' replied Phil with a little smile.

'But if I wrote to your father and explained—'

'It wouldn't be any good,' Phil told him. 'It isn't only that Daddy expects people to do as he tells them. It's partly because "the Honour of the House" is involved. When a guest comes to Ardfalloch he must be given of its best. That's the Gael's idea of hospitality.'

'I suppose you think I'm crazy,' said Gerald with a sigh.

'No, I don't,' she replied. 'You see I feel the same. I simply couldn't shoot a stag – nor a hind either – but it's illogical.'

'I don't know what you mean!'

She sat down on the broad window-seat and looked up at him gravely. 'I'll tell you,' she said. 'You've seen Malcolm's map, haven't you? The deer forest looks enormous, but there are only certain places where there is food. So it can only support a certain number of deer. Daddy and Malcolm know the exact number of deer (stags and hinds) which can live in comfort at Ard na Feidh.'

'Mac said you didn't mind shooting foxes,' said Gerald.

'I suppose you think that's illogical too,' Phil suggested. 'It is – in a way – but foxes are cruel. Foxes kill deer-calves and young lambs and chickens. A fox got into my hen-run and killed eleven pullets . . . and then jumped out and left them lying. I wouldn't have minded if he had killed one and taken it with him to feed his cubs. Foxes are much worse now because there are no rabbits for them to feed on,' added Phil with a sigh.

'You mean they all died of that rabbit disease? So the rabbit disease was a bad thing—'

'No, it was a good thing,' interrupted Phil. 'There's more good grass for the deer. It's awfully difficult to say what's good and what's bad. If you upset the balance by eliminating one pest you find you've encouraged another. You find that something unforeseen has happened – something you never thought of – and you've got to do something about it. That's why I kill foxes.'

'Do you shoot them with a gun?'

'No, with a small rifle – a .22 – I have to because they're a frightful nuisance and Daddy and Mac haven't time.'

There was a short silence. Then Gerald said, 'Tell me more about deer. I want to learn all I can. You've been here all your life so—'

'Yes, I've lived here all my life,' agreed Phil. 'I've seen what happens when the winter is long and hard. Six years ago there was a very long hard winter. The snow lay deep in the corries . . . and the corries are the places where the grass grows, the places where the stags find their food. If the snow lies deep it takes a long time to melt. That's the dangerous time. I went up with Daddy one morning and it was dreadful,' declared Phil, her eyes widening at the recollection. 'We found deer which had died of starvation. We found deer which were so weak that they couldn't get up and run away when they saw us. They were too weak to move when eagles attacked them. It was dreadful! And the worst of it was we couldn't do anything to help them. Daddy had to shoot them to put them out of their misery. It was the only thing to do. Daddy was so upset that he cried. His cheeks were wet with tears. I cried too. Oh, Gerald, it was so – so dreadful that I couldn't stop crying. I cried all night.'

'Your father shouldn't have taken you—'

'Yes, he should!' interrupted Phil. 'It was right to take me and let me see it. We ought not to shut our eyes to things that happen, however dreadful they are. Before that I had been silly – I hated it when they killed deer – but after I had seen what happened (seen with my own eyes) I understood.'

'Malcolm fed them this year.'

She nodded. 'Yes. He wasn't keen on it but Sir Walter told him how to do it. I came up here one morning with Malcolm and saw them enjoying the food. It was rather nice watching them, you know, but feeding deer isn't natural; it isn't really the answer. (I mean a deer forest should stand on its own feet.) And anyhow you can only do it for a few weeks in the year until the snow has melted and the grass is growing. You couldn't go on feeding deer all the time. For one thing it would be too expensive and, for another, there would be no stalking.'

'No stalking?' echoed Gerald in surprise.

'They would become quite tame, of course, and instead of running away from the scent of man they would gather round, waiting to be fed. See?'

'Yes, of course! I never thought of that.'

Phil continued, 'I'll tell you another horrible thing that happens when a forest becomes over-crowded: the deer come down from the hills and eat the crops – and the farmers shoot them! You can't blame the farmers (the crops are their livelihood) but some of the farmers haven't got rifles so they shoot the deer with shot-guns. That's awful because the deer are wounded and run away and die in agonies.'

'But you've got high fences to keep the deer from straying, haven't you?'

'We try to do that,' replied Phil. 'But if they're very hungry they get through somehow. I've seen whole fields of crops – mostly root crops – which have been eaten and trampled on and destroyed by hungry deer. So you see, Gerald, they must be killed to keep the balance right. They must be shot by people who know how to shoot. A shot through the heart is an easy death compared with starvation.'

'A deer forest is a big responsibility,' said Gerald thoughtfully.

'Yes, it is,' agreed Phil. 'If you own a deer forest you've got to look after it properly. It doesn't pay, of course – in fact it costs quite a lot of money, one way and another. You can let it for the season but it isn't very satisfactory because you never know what the people you let it to will do. Sometimes it's all right, and sometimes not. A deer forest is like . . . well, it's like a hen-run,' declared Phil, smiling at the ridiculous comparison. 'If you keep too many hens in a confined space they peck each other. If you keep too many pigs in a barn they eat each other's tails—'

'What!'

'They do, really,' nodded Phil. She added, 'Even a hedge has to be looked after properly. If you don't prune it every year it straggles all over the place.'

'A deer forest has to be pruned,' said Gerald thoughtfully. 'That's what you mean, isn't it?'

'Yes.'

'Sir Walter told me a bit – and lent me a book – but you've made it much clearer.'

'I'm glad,' said Phil. 'You're going out tomorrow, and you're going to enjoy it.'

'Well, perhaps.'

'Listen, Gerald! You must shoot one good stag. Kill him with a shot through his heart. That will satisfy everybody. You need never kill another.'

'You're making fun of me,' said Gerald smiling. 'But that's what I shall do . . . if I can.'

7 Which concerns itself with four good companions

The day following Gerald's arrival at Tigh na Feidh was dull and rainy; the visibility was too poor for stalking but the four young people arrayed themselves in rain-coats and walked up the path beside the burn.

Mac was disappointed – he had been looking forward to taking his new friend for a day's stalking – but Gerald did not mind.

There was something very pleasant about life at Tigh na Feidh. It was peaceful and easy-going and his companions were delightful. He was becoming more deeply in love with Phil every moment. Gerald was at the stage when it was a joy to watch her, to mark the graceful turn of her head, to listen to her voice. It was a pleasure to be of service to her, to fetch logs for the fire or open a door for her or to trim a lamp and to put it on the table by her side. Then she would look up and smile and thank him. (Later he would want more but for the moment this was enough.) He became fond of Mac, too. In fact, Gerald decided that Mac was one of the best fellows he had ever known in all his life.

Mac and Phil were devoted to each other – that was easily seen – sometimes they teased each other and occasionally, when they disagreed, they indulged in wordy warfare half in fun and half in earnest. Then suddenly one or other of them would begin to laugh . . . and it was all over in a moment.

He liked Donny Eastwood – nobody could help liking Donny – but she was so quiet and reserved that she remained a shadowy figure to Gerald.

The four had gone some way up the burn when they met Malcolm coming down and stopped to speak to him. He was carrying a string of small trout.

'I was just thinking these would be nice for your supper,' he explained.

'Oh, lovely!' cried Phil.

'You didn't get those on a rod,' declared Mac.

'That is so,' Malcolm agreed. He smiled and added, 'There are other ways of catching fish. You are knowing that, Mac! . . . or maybe you have forgotten what you used to be doing when you were a wee lad?'

'What about the weather?' inquired Mac anxiously.

'Och, it is not good,' the man replied. 'Tomorrow will be misty too, but it will clear when the wind changes. That is what I am thinking. Then we will be going out early and Mr Burleigh Brown will be killing his first stag.'

'Sickening, isn't it?' Mac exclaimed as they walked on. 'Last week we had splendid weather and now, when Gerald is here, down comes the mist. I'd like to take a huge broom and sweep it all away!'

There were two days of mist and rain, then on the Friday evening Malcolm came in to tell them that the wind had changed and tomorrow would be 'a grand day on the hill' and to ask if they wanted to start early.

'Yes, of course!' cried Mac. 'You're on, aren't you, Gerald? You don't mind getting up early?' He did not wait for Gerald's reply but followed Malcolm out of the room to make the necessary arrangements.

'Is Malcolm always right?' asked Gerald.

'Usually,' replied Phil. She smiled and added, 'If he happens to be wrong, once in a while, there's always a good reason for it. I mean it doesn't affect his confidence in himself.'

When Gerald awoke the next morning he saw that it was

still very misty and wondered whether this was one of the occasions when Malcolm was wrong, however he heard Mac whistling cheerfully in his room across the landing so he got up and dressed quickly, putting on the garments which Sir Walter had advised: old riding-breeches and khaki puttees and strong black boots with rubber soles. His brown leather jacket had weathered to a greenish tinge – he had worn it in Africa – so it was admirable for camouflage on a Scottish hillside. He went down to breakfast and found Mac already seated at the table wearing an old kilt, tattered and stained, a Harris jacket which had seen better days, thick grey stockings and nailed boots. Round his waist was a belt of khaki webbing in which he carried a telescope and a sheathed knife.

'What about the mist?' asked Gerald.

'It will clear,' replied Mac. 'Phil laughs at Malcolm but he's lived here all his life and nine times out of ten he's right about the weather.'

Old Kirsty had cooked breakfast – the girls had not come down – so the two young men ate quickly and, for a time, there was silence.

'Mac,' said Gerald at last. 'I'm rather scared about this business. As you know I've never shot deer before. I'm quite a good shot at a target but supposing I wound the creature? I'd really rather watch you shoot it.'

'We've all got to start,' Mac pointed out. 'And Dad said in his letter that you were to have the chance of killing a good stag. I know how you feel; I felt the same about my first stag: butterflies in the tummy?'

'Yes,' admitted Gerald.

'We may not see a stag – or have a chance to kill him. You realise that, don't you? But if we do I'll be ready to finish him off. Does that make you feel better?'

'Yes, a whole lot better,' said Gerald gratefully.

'All right then! But there's no need to say anything to Malcolm. See?'

Gerald nodded. The promise had taken a weight off his mind and he finished his breakfast with a better appetite.

The morning mist was still clinging to the hillside when the two set out together but before they had gone far the sun was struggling through – it looked like a big golden ball in the sky. Mac had arranged to meet Malcolm and the boy with the pony at a certain rock. From here they could ford the burn by some stepping-stones and strike upwards to the shoulder of the hill.

The mist did not trouble Mac, he knew the path too well. Gerald, following him, could hear the tinkle of the burn and, far away, the cry of a curlew, very faint and wild. Gerald was excited now. He was not so 'scared'. He hoped that he would be able to do what was expected of him. He must do exactly as he was told. That was the important thing.

'It's a pity we can't go different ways,' said Mac as he led the way to the rendezvous. 'But Malcolm wouldn't have it. Malcolm says Colin MacTaggart isn't experienced enough to stalk a stag – in fact Malcolm doesn't think Colin will ever be any use! But I'm not worrying too much about that.'

'Malcolm's standard is high,' suggested Gerald smiling.

'Yes, he expects too much. Colin is young and keen, he wants to do well which is more than half the battle. I like him,' continued Mac. 'He's a good lad. He supports his mother (who is a widow) and two young brothers who are still at school. Dad has given the family a cottage to live in. It's a very small cottage near the bridge – not much of a place but Mrs MacTaggart has done what she can with it. She wants to make "a nice home" for her boys.'

'Any relation of the innkeeper?' asked Gerald.

'Yes, Colin's father was his nephew – and I rather think

he helps them a bit – but all the same they're having a struggle to make ends meet. Colin's clothes are old and worn – there's not much warmth in them – but, although they're darned and patched, they're always clean and tidy. I feel sorry for them, Gerald.'

Gerald felt sorry for them too. He liked Colin; the boy had pleasant manners. He was tall and good-looking with bright red hair, a clear complexion and a shy smile which displayed excellent teeth. There was something very attractive about Colin MacTaggart and Gerald decided that at the end of his visit to Tigh na Feidh he would give Colin a substantial tip. (Gerald was getting a generous salary from Sir Walter so he could afford to be generous.)

Malcolm was waiting for them at the stepping-stones with the boy and the pony so they crossed the burn and set off up the hill.

'I thought you were bringing Colin,' said Mac. 'It would have been good experience for him.'

'He is no use, that one,' growled Malcolm.

'Give him time,' said Mac.

Almost at once the mist began to evaporate, a breeze sprang up and blew the melting shreds away and the hills stood up in bold ridges and jagged crests against the pale blue sky.

Mac had been talking to Malcolm but now he turned back to his guest. 'We're going to try the shoulder of Ben Ghaoth,' he said. 'It's a stiff climb but the stags are still on the high ground and we're pretty sure to find a good one up there.'

Gerald nodded. 'The air is marvellous; I could climb for hours without getting tired.'

'Good,' said Mac.

An hour's solid climbing brought them out of the heather on to the bare hillside. It was hot and shadeless so Gerald was glad when they turned the shoulder of the hill and felt the wind in their faces: it was a cool west wind from the Atlantic.

They left the boy and the pony in the shade of a rock and went on up a scree of loose stones. Gerald, looking back, saw the country spread before him like a map: forest and heather, lochs and tarns sparkling in the morning sunshine. It was a glorious view. He was glad he had seen Malcolm's map of Ard na Feidh for he was able to orient himself. He could see the green holm where the hinds found shelter, beyond that was the river and beyond the river was the road which divided Ard na Feidh from Glen Veigh. Just below the hill where he was standing there were heathery slopes and rough grassy hollows and screes of greyish black stones. He could see the funny little turrets peeping up from behind a rise in the ground and it struck him that perhaps Mac's great-great-grandfather had not added the turrets to Tigh na Feidh 'just for fun': a lantern, placed there on a dark night might guide a belated wanderer home. Perhaps, at this very minute, Phil was watching from the turret with a telescope . . . dear, sweet, beautiful Phil!

But this was no time to moon over Phil! His companions had gone on, so Gerald scrambled up the scree and found that they had reached the top of the slope and halted there. He saw now that this hill was not really the top but merely an excrescence on the shoulder of the mountain. The land dipped to a bog-filled dell and then rose, steeper and more rocky, to the mountain peak. Malcolm had taken out his telescope and was scanning the hills.

'Look you, Mac!' he was saying eagerly. 'Look you over toward Ben Ghaoth! There is a staggie at the entrance of the corrie where we killed the fourteen-pointer two years ago.'

Mac already had his telescope out and had rested it on a convenient rock so Gerald took Sir Walter's field glasses out of their leather case and focused them. For a few moments he could see nothing but the bare hillside, shimmering in the heat-haze that rose from the damp ground, but presently he caught sight of something brown, something that moved . . .

Mac had seen it too. 'Yes, it's a stag,' he said.

'It is a very big stag,' declared Malcolm. 'It is too far to see his points but he is a good-sized beast – so he is!'

'There's your stag, Gerald,' said Mac.

Between the stalkers and their quarry lay the boggy declivity and a steep hillside covered with boulders and loose stones – a difficult approach! If they were to dislodge a stone they might start a small avalanche which would warn the stag of their approach. Malcolm explained this to Gerald, adding that one thing in their favour was the direction of the wind. It was blowing directly in their faces so there was no chance of the beast getting their scent. Deer have such a keen sense of smell that they can scent a man from an incredibly long distance and one whiff, borne by a vagrant breeze, will send them bounding away over the hills.

'They scent you before they can see you,' explained Mac.

'Come,' said Malcolm, shutting his telescope and starting off.

Gerald followed him and Mac brought up the rear. The boggy patch presented no difficulties but when they had climbed up the other side it was not so easy to walk quietly. (The stones crunched beneath their feet and rattled down the slope), but fortunately the ground soon became more level and was knit together by tufts of coarse yellow grass. Gerald noticed that Malcolm was walking on these tufts and avoiding the bare patches so he was careful to place his feet in the man's footprints.

By this time they had descended the hillock in an oblique direction and had lost sight of the stag. Its position was marked by a piled up mass of black igneous rock. Malcolm stopped here and signed to his companions to wait while he reconnoitred. Then he swung himself up and disappeared.

Gerald and Mac waited without speaking. It was very still. Not a blade of grass moved – for they were sheltered from the wind – not a creature stirred. The sun beat down, warming their backs. The rocks were hot to the touch.

It seemed to Gerald that they waited a long time, but probably it was only a few minutes, then Malcolm reappeared and made a signal to them.

Gerald did not understand what he meant but Mac had dropped on to his hands and knees and was creeping round the corner of the rocks, so Gerald followed his example . . . and presently they found themselves on a stony ridge looking down into a narrow valley. A small burn ran down the middle of the valley, zigzagging its way between stones. There was no sign of the stag; he seemed to have vanished into thin air.

'He has moved into the upper part of the corrie,' Malcolm whispered.

'Are you sure?' asked Mac.

Malcolm nodded. 'I saw him go, but he moved slowly and quietly. He was not frightened at all. He will be there, feeding – that is what I am thinking.'

Gerald looked up the little valley and saw that it narrowed to a cleft in the hills. From here the burn fell in a miniature waterfall over a flat rock. There was a passage between the burn and the cliff's edge, a narrow path masked by a huge black boulder.

'We could try the top part,' Malcolm whispered. 'It is a favourite place, for the burn rises there and the grass is sweet and good. The corrie widens out above the bend.'

'Yes,' agreed Mac. 'The only thing is he might get our scent if we go up that way. Could we go back and come at him from the top?'

Malcolm considered this. At last he said, 'I doubt if we

could get near enough – and it is a difficult thing to be shooting a stag from above. I am thinking we will need to risk him getting our scent and follow him up the burn.'

'We'll risk it,' nodded Mac.

They went down to the burn as silently as possible, crossed it and climbed up the opposite bank. It took them several minutes to reach the little waterfall. Gerald could now see that the passage between the burn and the cliff was less narrow than he had thought, for the boulder stood in front of the opening, not flush with it.

Malcolm knelt down and examined the damp sod very carefully. 'Yes, he has come this way,' he whispered. 'There are his slots . . . but I am a wee bit puzzled, Mac.'

'Why? What's the matter?'

'It is just that he is a heavier beast than I thought.'

'Well, it doesn't matter, does it?' said Mac impatiently. 'Let's get on, Malcolm.'

Malcolm nodded and rose. 'We'll climb up the cliff. You will be getting a better chance at him that way.'

The three of them scrambled up the side of the cliff. It was warm with the sun and its crevices were filled with tufts of grass and ferns and little pools of water. From the top of the cliff they could see into the top part of the corrie – a small valley filled with boulders which had fallen from the mountain. Between the boulders the grass was green and lush.

A stag was grazing quietly amongst the boulders, quite unaware of their approach.

8 Which describes the slaying of a stag

Gerald could sense his companions' excitement. It was the excitement of the hunter when he sees his quarry within his grasp. Gerald's feeling was different: there, before his eyes, was the creature which he was obliged to kill. He was obliged to kill it – if he could. He had no option. There was no getting out of it now. If it had been a 'switch' he would not have minded (there were good reasons for killing a switch) but this was no switch. This was a beautiful graceful creature, a stag in his prime with ten – yes, ten – points to his branching antlers.

All this had flashed through Gerald's head in a moment, meanwhile he had taken up his position: he had spread out his legs and settled his rifle on a jutting piece of rock. Mac lay down beside him, ready to keep his word.

The stag was about a hundred and twenty yards away – an easy shot – but he was grazing towards them, head on.

'Wait,' breathed Mac.

Gerald waited. He realised that the stag might sense their presence and be off like an arrow from a bow, but there might be a few seconds when he would stand still with his head lifted, sniffing the air. That would be Gerald's chance.

I must do it, Gerald decided. If I do it properly, if I shoot him clean through the heart, I need never do it again. This will be my first stag . . . and my last. Having made this decision he felt better: his heart, which had been thumping uncomfortably, slowed down and his breath came more easily.

The stag went on grazing. It was so still and sheltered in the corrie that Gerald could hear the click of the creature's hoof against a stone. He was coming nearer very slowly, seeking out the tender green grass between the boulders.

Suddenly the stag raised his head . . . and listened. His glistening brown body turned sideways, he sniffed the air. By this time he was a hundred yards away – not more.

Gerald aimed just behind the shoulder. The shot rang out, crisp and clear, startling the echoes, and the stag bounded into the air. Gerald thought he had missed – but he had not missed! After one bound towards the burn, the beast rolled over, his four feet beat the air for a few moments, then all was still.

'Oh, good work!' exclaimed Mac in delight. 'Oh, well done, Gerald!'

He had scarcely spoken when a huge brown beast bounded up from behind a boulder and fled madly across the corrie.

'Shoot, man!' cried Malcolm excitedly. 'Shoot, Mac – for Gaud's sake shoot!'

Mac hesitated with his finger on the trigger of his rifle. 'But Malcolm, it's a hind!' he exclaimed.

By this time the beast had sprung across the burn with one enormous leap – an incredible leap – and was half-way up the other side of the corrie, its hooves clattering amongst the loose stones and sending small avalanches of stones down the steep slope. It was well out of range now so Mac took his eyes off it, and turned to look at Malcolm.

'Och, Mac, why did you not shoot?' lamented Malcolm. 'Yon was no hind! It was a great big ugly hummel! Och, Mac, you should have shot when I was telling you!'

'Good heavens! Are you sure?'

'Am I sure? Have you ever seen a hind that size? The brute had buttocks like a horse! It was all of twenty stone – aye, it was more!'

'Oh, well, it's gone now,' said Mac.

'Aye, it's gone,' agreed Malcolm sorrowfully. 'And dear knows when we will be seeing it again.'

He rose as he spoke and leapt down from the rock to gralloch the kill.

Gerald followed. He was glad he had done it successfully.

Mac followed his companions more slowly. He was upset about the hummel and realised he had been a fool not to shoot when Malcolm had told him: he should have trusted Malcolm. The loss of the hummel had taken the edge off his pleasure at Gerald's success, but it was no use crying over spilt milk. Gerald had done well – he couldn't have done better – he must be given his due meed of praise.

Malcolm had taken out his tape measure and was measuring the stag's antlers.

'It is not a big head,' Malcolm was saying. 'But it is a very perfect one. You will not be seeing a more perfect ten-pointer for a long time, Mr Burleigh Brown. Look you, the tines are beautifully shaped above and below.'

'Yes,' agreed Mac. 'It's a beautiful head. Your first stag, Gerald! You got him straight through the heart. It was a fine shot wasn't it, Malcolm?'

'It was well-judged,' agreed Malcolm . . . and indeed he was satisfied. Mr Burleigh Brown had waited in patience until the right moment and then had shot without hesitation. It was a good performance for a novice.

Gerald said nothing. He had put his hand on the creature's neck, the fur was soft and warm to the touch. Ten minutes ago the creature had been alive. Now it was dead. ('I'm sorry, old chap,' said Gerald inwardly. 'I had to do it.') Aloud he said, 'He's a beautiful creature. Can you tell how old he is, Malcolm?'

'He would be about eleven years old,' replied Malcolm.

'He is in his prime. When a stag is past fourteen he will be going downhill, just as a man who is past forty. This head is worth mounting, Mr Burleigh Brown.'

'Yes, that's right,' agreed Mac. 'We'll send it off to the taxidermist in Inverness tomorrow morning. I must write to Dad and tell him about it. He'll be pleased. Sir Walter will be pleased, too.' He added, 'It's nearly three o'clock and I'm as hungry as a wolf. Let's sit down in the shade of the cliff and eat our sandwiches.'

They sat down together and opened their packet of sandwiches.

'I was ready but you didn't need any help,' said Mac.

'It was a help,' replied Gerald. 'The knowledge that you were standing by steadied me.'

'You were as cool as a cucumber!'

'Not really.'

Gerald had not felt hungry but now that he had begun to eat his sandwiches he discovered that he was . . . and he was beginning to feel a good deal better. 'Hullo!' he added in surprise. 'What is Malcolm doing?'

Mac looked up and saw that Malcolm had collected some sticks and dry grass.

'Is he going to cook the liver for his dinner?' asked Gerald.

'Good heavens, no!' exclaimed Mac, roaring with laughter. 'Malcolm is much too civilised. He's going to send up a smoke signal for the boy to bring the pony, that's all.'

Gerald laughed too. 'How silly of me! I might have guessed that was what he was doing.'

'It wasn't silly,' said Mac quickly. 'You couldn't possibly know what he was doing. It was just that I couldn't help laughing at the idea of Malcolm cooking the stag's liver – and eating it. Malcolm has no opinion of venison as food. Not even when his mother cooks it and hands it to him on a plate! Of course you're used to camping out (you've done it in Africa, haven't you?) so it was quite a natural mistake.'

Gerald realised that Mac wanted to put him in the right – and he was rather touched. There was something very charming and boyish about Mac. He was intuitive and considerate; he was extraordinarily kind. I don't know when I've met any man I like so much, thought Gerald.

Malcolm had finished cleaning the stag and, having washed his hands in the burn, sat down a little way off to have his lunch.

'Tell me, Mac,' said Gerald in a low voice. 'I want to know more about that hummel. I suppose the reason Malcolm was so upset about losing the creature was the fact that calves sired by a hummel are unlikely to have horns.'

'Very unlikely to have good horns, anyway,' Mac replied. He smiled and added, 'Malcolm will give us no peace until the beast is dead.'

'It was strange seeing it.'

'Yes, I was surprised. He must have been lying in the shade of that big boulder, sleeping or chewing the cud. Your shot scared him.'

'He was a large brute.'

'They often are. Some people think it's because they don't grow horns every year – as other stags do – so all their strength goes into their bodies. Others say it's because they're so easily mistaken for hinds.' Mac raised his voice and called to Malcolm: 'Malcolm, have you ever seen that hummel before?'

'I have not,' replied Malcolm promptly. 'He would not be living now if I had been seeing him before. I would have put an end to him myself. We must see and kill him before the rut starts.'

'Where can he have come from?'

'He will have come over the river from Glen Veigh.'

Mac and Gerald smiled at each other: everything bad 'came over the river from Glen Veigh'!

'Couldn't a hummel just be a freak?' asked Gerald.

'I suppose it might happen,' Malcolm replied. 'But, to my mind, it's unlikely. Besides yon hummel is not a young beast. I would have been seeing him before if he had grown from a calf in my forest. I am about the place at all seasons of the year – not like Mackenzie who sits by the fire on his backside for the most part of the winter,' added Malcolm scornfully.

Soon after this the boy arrived with the pony; the carcass of the stag was lifted and strapped securely on to the pony's back.

'It looks too heavy for that small pony,' Gerald remarked.

'These small Shetlands are very sturdy,' Mac told him. In fact they're ideal for the job. They're hardy and sure-footed and very wise. One day we were right over the other side of Ben Ghaoth and a mist came down. It came suddenly and unexpectedly and it was so thick that you couldn't see a yard. Even Malcolm, who knows the forest like the palm of his hand, was doubtful about getting home . . . not so Queenie! She set off quite confidently and brought us home over the hills by the shortest way. It's amazing what strong instincts these creatures have.'

The little cavalcade started off. Malcolm and the boy and the pony in front, Mac and Gerald following . . . and talking.

'Did you enjoy your day?' Mac asked.

'I enjoyed the stalking, it was grand fun and very interesting indeed, but I didn't enjoy killing that lovely animal.'

'You didn't enjoy it? But you did it splendidly!'

'I did it because I had to,' Gerald explained. 'I suppose I'm different from other men, but, quite honestly, I don't want to kill another.'

'You don't want to kill another?'

'No.'

'But Gerald—'

'Oh, I'll shoot switches and I'm quite willing to shoot that hummel if we see it, but—'

'Didn't it give you a thrill? I remember my first stag: I was fifteen and I was out with Dad and Malcolm and Sir Walter MacCallum. It was a hot day (not a breath of wind) and we had done no good. The stags were restless. We had seen three and had toiled after them, uphill and downhill for hours. I was tired and bored and I had a blister on my heel which was giving me hell. Then, quite unexpectedly, we came upon a nine-point stag grazing quietly in a little quarry. Malcolm gave the signal for us to lie down, so down we went behind a bank with heather on the top of it. Sir Walter was lying beside me – it had been decided that if we got within range of a good stag he was to kill it – but instead of shooting the beast he turned his head and smiled at me and put his rifle into my hands. I had shot with his rifle before, but only at a target, so I couldn't believe he meant me to kill the stag. I looked at him and he looked at me – and nodded. I was shaking all over with excitement and my hands were wet with perspiration but somehow or other I pulled myself together and took careful aim and shot. The stag bounded for a few yards – I thought I had missed – then it rolled over and over down the slope and lay still. Sir Walter patted my back and said, "Well done, laddie!" so then I knew it was all right.

'It was an easy shot, of course,' explained Mac. 'That was why Sir Walter had given it to me – but I had done it. I had killed my first stag! Oh, I was wild with delight! I could have sung and danced with joy. I felt like a king.'

'I don't blame you,' Gerald told him. 'I just feel differently, that's all. My stag was a beautiful creature; he was alive and free; he was grazing happily; he had no idea that he had an enemy lurking behind a rock. Five minutes later he was a dead body, a carcass lying on the ground. I don't expect you to understand. We'll just have to agree that I'm a freak.'

They looked at each other – and laughed – and went on down the hill in complete harmony.

9 Introduces another guest at the House of the Deer

When Gerald and Mac returned from the hill Kirsty told them that 'Mr Stoddart' had arrived and was having tea with the two young ladies.

'Oh, good!' said Mac. 'I told you about Oliver Stoddart, didn't I, Gerald? Come on in and meet him.'

'I'll have a bath first – if you don't mind,' replied Gerald (he had no wish to sit down at table dirty and dishevelled).

'Right oh!' said Mac cheerfully. Then he arranged with Malcolm to send the stag's head to Inverness the following morning, and a haunch of venison to Sir Walter Mac-Callum, and went in to greet the new guest.

They all looked up when he went in, but it was Phil who spoke first. 'Hullo!' she exclaimed. 'You're back earlier than I expected. We didn't wait for you because Oliver was hungry.'

'Hullo, Oliver! How are you?' said Mac. 'I expect Phil has told you we've got a guest.'

'Yes,' replied Oliver.

'How did you get on?' asked Phil. 'Did you have a good day?'

'Yes, splendid,' replied Mac. 'Couldn't have been better. Gerald did awfully well.' He turned to Oliver and added, 'Gerald Burleigh Brown – he's a great chap – he has never done any stalking before but he's got the idea all right. He killed his first stag today.'

'Oh!' exclaimed Phil in delight. 'Oh, I hope it was a good one?'

'A ten-pointer – a beautiful head! I'm having it mounted

for him. He really did awfully well,' repeated Mac, sitting down at the table. 'Nobody could have guessed that it was his first day on the hill. He behaved like an old hand and was as cool as a cucumber: waited his chance and got the beast clean through the heart. Even Malcolm was pleased with his performance and said it was "well-judged".'

Phil smiled. She was aware that this, from Malcolm, was the highest praise possible.

They went on talking about it. Oliver listened in silence, his face set in obstinate lines. He had been annoyed to discover that there was another guest at Tigh na Feidh for he knew that the MacAslans could not afford more than one good stalker and it meant that he, himself, would not get so much sport . . . and, in addition to this, he was the kind of young man who prefers to be praised, rather than to hear of other young men's achievements! Last, but by no means least, it appeared to him that Phil was more interested in this new friend than she should be.

Oliver had known Phil for years of course; he had always looked upon her as a young sister; somebody who need not be considered very much! He enjoyed his bachelor life and the comforts provided for him by his doting mother.

Oliver was tall and good-looking with a pronounced wave in his fair hair. He shot well, danced well, and owned an exceedingly comfortable car so he was able to amuse himself very pleasantly with the young women of his acquaintance . . . but just lately (for some reason or other) these simple pleasures had begun to pall and he had decided to get married. It was a big step to take and he debated it with himself, suggesting and rejecting various estimable young women who, he was assured, would accept him without hesitation. Finally he thought of Phil MacAslan.

There was no money there, of course (the MacAslans were as poor as church mice) but Oliver had enough money already. And there were advantages in an alliance with the family: not only would he be able to get good sport at Ardfalloch whenever he liked but, as MacAslan's son-in-law, he would be *persona grata* with other big landowners in the district.

Thus it was that when Oliver arrived at Tigh na Feidh he looked at Phil with new eyes and saw at once how right he had been. She really was an attractive creature. Yes, thought Oliver, she was the very girl he wanted. So it was rather a blow to find a strange man in the house and to find that Phil seemed to be 'interested' in him. It was rather a blow . . . well, perhaps not exactly a 'blow', thought Oliver, because of course it would make no difference in the long run. Phil was a sensible girl and would realise her good fortune in having attracted such an eligible suitor as Oliver Stoddart.

Meanwhile Mac was feeling worried. Oliver seemed to be in one of his mulish moods. He had shown no enthusiasm over the story of this morning's sport. It would have been natural to say: 'Oh, good show!' or something like that when Mac had explained about Gerald killing his first stag – any man would have said it! Mac was not used to dealing with difficult situations. His two guests were both older than himself and if they did not mix well it would be ghastly. Mac wished – not for the first time – that his father were here.

Phil continued to chat . . . and she was so pleased at Gerald's success which (quite rightly) she attributed to her talk with him that she was unable to leave the subject alone. They had finished tea by this time so they moved over to the big chairs by the fire.

'It *was* good, wasn't it?' said Phil, taking up a grey stocking which she had been darning.

'It was wonderful,' agreed Donny enthusiastically.

'What was wonderful?' asked Oliver.

'I've just been telling you,' said Mac. 'Perhaps you weren't listening. This was Gerald's first day on the hill and he killed a ten-pointer – shot it clean through the heart.'

Oliver hesitated. He had listened of course, but he had not been interested. He saw now that he should have shown a little enthusiasm for the exploit. His ill humour had done him no good so perhaps it would be better to be civil about it.

'I wasn't really listening,' he explained. 'I've driven miles today and I was hungry. I think you said that this was your friend's first day at Ard na Feidh.'

'It was his first day's stalking,' said Mac (pleased that Oliver seemed to be emerging from his gloom). 'It was his first day and his first stag. He has shot lions of course.'

Phil and Donny both looked up in astonishment.

'Lions?' asked Oliver incredulously.

Mac was smiling: he had just remembered this interesting fact. 'Yes, when he was in Africa,' said Mac.

'I don't believe it,' declared Oliver.

'You don't believe it?'

'No, I don't,' said Oliver, lying back in his chair and crossing his legs in a nonchalant manner. 'You wouldn't believe it either if you knew the first thing about big game shooting. My friend, Lucius Cottar, has done a lot of big game shooting and he told me all about it.'

'But Oliver—'

'Big game shooting in Africa isn't all that easy,' declared Oliver, raising his voice and paying no attention to Mac's interruption. 'You can't just take a rifle and go out and shoot a lion. You've got to get a permit; you've got to join a safari expedition and buy a lot of expensive equipment; you've got to hire boys to carry the stuff; you've got to—'

'I don't know anything about all that! I only know that Gerald has shot lions.'

'How do you know?'

'He told me so himself.'

'He was having you on, old boy,' said Oliver smiling in a supercilious manner.

'Do you mean he was lying?'

'You can put it like that if you like.'

'How else can you put it?' asked Mac heatedly. 'You say he's a liar. Well, he happens to be a friend of mine and I say he isn't.'

'Oliver didn't mean that,' put in Donny, trying to pour oil on the troubled waters.

'What did he mean?' asked Mac.

'If Gerald told Mac he had shot lions in Africa he *did*!' cried Phil. 'You can ask him of course—'

'I shall,' said Oliver.

It was at this moment that the door opened and Gerald came in. He had had his bath and looked clean and cool and comfortable in grey flannel slacks and a blue pullover. He was a little surprised to find a somewhat strained atmosphere in the room . . . and dead silence.

10 In which Donny becomes communicative

Phil was the first to recover. She jumped to her feet and introduced the guests to each other, adding hastily: 'Go on, Mac. You can show Oliver his room; it's all ready for him. I'll make fresh tea for Gerald.'

'Yes, of course!' agreed Mac. 'Come on Oliver. Where's your suitcase?'

The two men went off together, Phil fled to the kitchen and Donny came and sat down at the table beside Gerald.

'What was all that?' asked Gerald smiling at her.

'Oh, nothing much! Oliver is rather a bore, that's all. Of course you don't know him yet, do you?'

Gerald agreed that he did not . . . though, as a matter of fact, he had sized up his fellow guest in one cool glance: rich and good-looking, rather spoilt and a bit too pleased with himself would have been his verdict on his fellow guest.

'Do you like it here?' asked Donny.

'Yes, it's a lovely place.'

'It's like heaven,' said Donny dreamily. 'It's quite, quite perfect.'

Gerald was a little surprised to find Donny Eastwood communicative. He had liked her, of course, but so far she had spoken very seldom and had merely listened and smiled when the others were talking.

'Perhaps you think it's silly,' continued Donny. 'But really and truly Tigh na Feidh seems like heaven to me: the hills and the burns and the peacefulness and to be able to do what you like all the time: to talk or not talk; to be a little untidy; to go out for a walk and come in late – and make tea and have it when you want it – but principally to be with Phil and Mac. Phil is marvellous. You think so too, don't you?'

'Yes,' said Gerald.

'They're so kind,' continued Donny. 'They're so good to me – and they don't think I'm silly.'

'You aren't silly.'

'Not here,' she agreed. 'I'm quite clever when I'm here. When people think you're silly it makes you sillier.'

Gerald agreed with this for he had had much the same experience. He had been rather a fool. Then he had gone to stay with Bess in her London flat. She had cured him. She had made him feel clever. He explained this to Donny.

'That's very interesting,' said Donny, looking at him with soft dove's eyes. 'I thought perhaps I was the only person to feel like that – but you understand!'

'Yes,' said Gerald nodding.

'Bess is your sister, isn't she? I read about her in the papers and saw her photographs. I wish I could have seen her on the stage but of course I couldn't. I've often wondered whether she ever regrets leaving the stage and becoming an everyday sort of person.'

'She doesn't,' Gerald replied. 'She's perfectly happy. She made a success on the stage and she's making a success of everyday life.'

'Do you wish she were here, Gerald?'

Gerald hesitated. This was a very penetrating question. He was devoted to Bess; ever since he was a small boy he had loved Bess best in all the world. He still loved her dearly – not a bit less – but, somehow, he didn't wish she were here.

'Don't answer if you'd rather not,' said Donny hastily. 'I shouldn't have asked, of course. I just wondered, that was all.' She sighed and added, 'It won't be quite so nice now, you know.'

There was no need to ask what she meant.

'We shall have to help them,' Donny continued. 'I mean help Mac and Phil. They aren't used to being patient and – and tactful. They're used to saying what they feel straight out.'

'I like that,' Gerald told her.

'Oh, so do I!' agreed Donny. 'People who have no fire in them are awfully stodgy. Phil and Mac often quarrel, you know. I mean they quarrel with each other. I used to be rather frightened but then I realised that they were so fond of each other that it didn't matter. Now I sit on the fence and listen – and hold their coats! Then suddenly they begin to laugh and it's all over in a minute. Oliver Stoddart is quite different. If people don't agree with him he gets angry and sulks.'

There was a short silence.

At last Gerald said, 'Perhaps he won't stay long.'

'He'll stay as long as he gets "good sport" – or until someone sends him an invitation that sounds more attractive,' replied Donny. 'And I think his friends are beginning to get rather tired of him. I don't know whether he's getting more didactic as he gets older or because the more you see of him the less you like him. I'm sorry for him,' she added.

Gerald agreed that Mr Stoddart was to be pitied. The reverse was true of Donny Eastwood. Gerald had begun by thinking she was a nice quiet girl – but rather dull – and now he found himself liking her very much indeed.

'Have you brothers or sisters?' he asked.

'Two brothers – Harold and Barney. They're both younger than I am and they escaped in time.'

'Escaped?' asked Gerald.

She nodded. 'Yes, they were rather stupid when they were little but they got away in time and now they're quite clever. Barney is the lucky one. He fell down a cliff and broke his leg terribly badly so he'll always be lame. I know it sounds queer but it really was very lucky indeed because he has got exactly what he wanted, so he doesn't mind being lame. You can't have everything, can you?'

'What happened?' asked Gerald.

'We were staying at Targ with the MacRynnes (Tessa MacRynne was my best friend at school) and it was when we were there that the accident happened. It was nobody's fault, of course, but Colonel MacRynne took the responsibility for it and offered to have Barney trained to be his factor and to help him to look after his estate. Colonel MacRynne owns a great deal of property so he really needs someone to help him – and Barney adores Colonel Mac-Rynne so he's terribly happy about it.' Donny smiled and added, 'You see what I meant when I said it was lucky that he broke his leg so badly.'

Gerald saw. He said, 'Well, that's Barney settled. What about Harold?'

'Harold is quite different,' Donny replied. 'He's much more serious than Barney. He's very good at figures so he's going to be a Chartered Accountant. It's a very difficult exam, you know.'

'I know,' agreed Gerald.

'But he's working terribly hard so I'm sure he'll pass . . . And I was just wondering if he could get a post in Sir Walter MacCallum's Shipyard?'

'I'll make a point of speaking to Sir Walter about him.'

'Oh, that *would* be kind!'

'It wouldn't be "kind",' replied Gerald smiling. 'If Harold passes his exam, he'll be able to get a good post anywhere: Chartered Accountants don't grow on every bush.'

'He's a good boy,' said Donny earnestly. 'He really is very good and conscientious and – and persevering but I'm his sister so naturally I think he's marvellous.'

Harold's sister had become quite pink with excitement in talking about him . . . and Gerald noticed that she was a great deal prettier than he had thought. In fact she was a very pretty girl (not beautiful like Phil, of course, but really very attractive). He soothed her down and assured her that Harold Eastwood sounded just the sort of chap that Sir Walter liked to get hold of. Young and keen and persevering. 'Tell him to write to me,' said Gerald. 'I'll make an appointment for him. That's the best way.'

As a matter of fact Gerald was rather intrigued by the story of Donny's brothers. She had said they had 'escaped'; they had 'got away in time'. He wondered what they had escaped from and was about to inquire further into the matter when the door opened and Oliver Stoddart came in . . . and Donny shut up like a clam.

11 Which concerns a shopping expedition

Early breakfast was the rule at the House of the Deer. Sometimes the girls had theirs later, but Mac was always early and so was Gerald . . . and today Oliver Stoddart was there too. He was sitting at the table demolishing a plateful of bacon and eggs when Gerald came downstairs.

'It's no good today,' Mac was saying.

'No good? What do you mean?' asked Oliver. 'You said I could have Malcolm today.'

'So you could,' agreed Mac. 'But there's mist on the hill; the visibility is too bad for stalking.'

'It's clearing,' objected Oliver. 'The mist is rising.'

'Malcolm says it's coming down. Oh, it may clear in the afternoon but that will be too late. I'm sorry, Oliver, but it really isn't any good when there's mist on Ben Ghaoth. You know that yourself.'

Gerald changed the subject hastily by saying that he intended to walk down to Ardfalloch village this morning and asking if there were any commissions to be done.

'You can get a paper,' said Mac. 'And you can call for the letters at the post office. I'd come with you if I could but I must write to Dad: I want his advice about several matters which can't be decided without him. I wish he were here,' added Mac with a sigh.

'I want razor blades,' said Oliver. 'I can't use my electric razor here. You ought to install an engine and have the house wired. It would be much more convenient.'

'Too expensive,' said Mac crossly.

'It wouldn't cost much. My friend Lucius Cottar makes his own electricity. He has an engine that runs on oil. I could ask him about it.'

'We couldn't afford it,' declared Mac more crossly than before. Then he rose and stumped out of the room.

' "Penny wise and pound foolish",' muttered Oliver. 'If this house were put in proper order they could let the forest every season and get a lot of money for it.'

'They wouldn't want to let it every season,' Gerald pointed out. Then (before Oliver could reply) he too rose and went to get ready for his walk.

Tigh na Feidh was so cut off from the outside world that nearly everybody wanted something in the village so Gerald was given a list of commissions. He was a little surprised at the variety of the things that were wanted and inquired somewhat anxiously if the shop (which adjoined the post office) would be able to supply them.

'Oh yes,' said Phil. 'Mrs Grant has everything that anybody could possibly want. It may take her some time to find them, but you won't mind that, will you?'

Gerald replied that he did not mind at all. Phil's requirements included a shampoo powder to wash her hair – naturally this came first on the list! Gerald decided that if Mrs Grant could not supply shampoo powder he would take his car and scour the country for it.

Mac saw him off at the door and explained that there was a short cut to the village, a steep path down the hill which led to a plantation of pine trees. 'There's no bridge across the river,' added Mac. 'The nearest bridge is the hump-backed bridge – that's a mile farther downstream but there are stepping-stones which will take you across dry-shod if the water isn't too high. We intend to put a light wooden bridge across the river one of these days but there never seems to be enough money for the job.'

'Don't worry. I'll get across somehow,' said Gerald – and with that he strode off down the hill.

The thought of wet feet did not worry Gerald, nor did the gentle misty rain which had begun to fall. He had spent so long in Africa that he rather enjoyed the rain . . . and he had put on a khaki rain-coat so he was equipped for any weather. The rain-coat was a peculiar garment (he had bought it in Johannesburg); it was old and faded and stained with red mud but that was a mere detail. Nobody in Ardfalloch would care.

The object of Gerald's expedition this morning was to find out if there was a woman in the village who could knit him a pair of thick grey stockings like the ones Mac had been wearing. He, himself, had been wearing puttees for stalking but they were hot and uncomfortable. At first he had put them on too tightly and then, when he had loosened them, they had flapped round his ankles. Stockings would be much easier.

At first the path was very steep and stony but presently it took a turn round an outcrop of rock and broadened into a cart-track where there was a high wire fence. Beyond the fence was the plantation of pine trees. Gerald found the gate and shut it carefully behind him (he realised that the fence was there to protect the trees from the depredations of deer). The pines were about ten feet high, they stood in neat rows like a regiment of soldiers. No doubt they were a valuable crop and would be 'harvested' when they reached maturity, but you would have to wait a long time for your money!

The path went on down the hill for about half a mile. Then there was another fence and a gate which led to a clearing beside the river . . . and here, in this little sheltered corner, there was a group of oaks. They were old and gnarled with twisted branches but in spite of their age they seemed healthy for their foliage was green and thick. Perhaps this was because they were growing so close to the water.

These were the first hardwood trees that Gerald had seen in the vicinity so he stopped to look at them. He wondered how they had come there and whether they were the survivors of a large forest. He must ask Mac their history – or perhaps he should ask Phil. Phil was sure to know.

Just beyond the oaks Gerald found the stepping-stones (they were quite dry today) so he crossed the river and scrambled up the opposite bank on to the road. Ten minutes' brisk walk brought him to Ardfalloch village.

Mrs Grant lived up to her reputation. She produced everything Gerald wanted, including the all-important shampoo powder, but these goods were so mixed up with a number of articles which Gerald did not want that he had quite a long time to wait for his parcel to be made up. Mrs Grant had electric light bulbs, brass door-knockers, postcards, fountain pens, headache powders, babies' rattles, seed potatoes, inkstands made of deers' horns, penwipers, artificial flowers, roller skates, sun-glasses, water pistols and boxes of fireworks all mixed up with knitted goods.

It was while Gerald was sitting upon the sack of seed potatoes – and marvelling at the diversity of Mrs Grant's stock – that his eye fell upon a white Shetland shawl. It was a delicious garment, as light as a feather and as fine as lace . . . so he bought it for Margaret. He would have bought a postcard to send to Bess but unfortunately the only ones left on the stand depicted Mont Blanc, the Statue of Liberty, the Eiffel Tower and the beach at Margate . . . all of which seemed unsuitable to despatch from Ardfalloch.

'How do you get all these things?' Gerald inquired.

'From my husband's second cousin's father-in-law,' Mrs Grant replied. 'He has an emporium in Chicago and sends me a crate of articles he is not wanting. He sends it twice a year so I am always well-stocked. Would Miss Phil be interested in a mud-pack for her complexion? Mud-packs are all the go in Chicago.'

'Miss Phil's complexion is perfect,' replied her admirer.

'Well, maybe you are right,' agreed Mrs Grant.

Mrs Grant tied up the parcel and Gerald stowed it away in the knapsack which he had brought with him. Then he paid for the goods. He was surprised to find that his purchases were so cheap.

'Have you included the shawl?' he asked.

'Oh, I am not charging much for the shawl,' replied Mrs Grant, smiling. 'It is just what I am doing to amuse myself in my spare time. I am very fond of babies.'

This seemed a curious idea to Gerald, however he could do nothing about it . . . so he thanked Mrs Grant and said goodbye.

Then he called at MacTaggart's Inn.

12 In which Gerald makes new friends

Mr MacTaggart was in the bar, polishing glasses, but he was never too busy for a chat so he greeted Gerald warmly and offered him one on the house.

'I am busy today,' he said. 'There is a meeting of the Ardfalloch Fire Brigade tonight so we will be having drinks when it is over. Talking is dry work.'

'You're the Captain, aren't you?' said Gerald, who had just remembered this interesting fact.

'That is so,' agreed Mr MacTaggart. He put down the glass which he had been polishing, leant his elbows on the counter and continued confidentially. 'We are not exactly official, Mister Gerald. It was like this, you see. There was a fire in the stables at Glen Veigh and before the Brigade from Kincraig was arriving the building was badly damaged, so one of the lads – it was Euan Dalgliesh – was saying it would be a good thing if we were having a Brigade of our own. The others were all for it. The only trouble was how to get the money. I was asking Mr Ross and he was all for it too. He was giving us a cheque for a hundred pounds – he is a very fine gentleman, is Mr Ross. So then we got together – me and some of the lads – and we bought a second-hand engine and brass helmets and such-like (just on our own, Mister Gerald). So far,' said Mr MacTaggart regretfully, 'so far there has only been stacks and barns for us to be practising on but we are always hoping for a real good blaze.'

Gerald hid a smile. He said, 'It was a good idea—'

'It was, indeed!' interrupted Mr MacTaggart. 'It was

Euan's idea, but if it had not been for me they would never have got much further. It is good to have ideas but you need somebody like me to carry them out.'

'You're the big fish,' suggested Gerald.

'I am the big fish,' agreed Mr MacTaggart, smiling all over his plump face. 'Everybody comes to me when they are wanting something done – or when they are wanting advice. They say, "Ask Jamie MacTaggart: he is sure to know." So they ask me why their hens are not laying and what time the bus goes to Kincraig and how they should vote at the General Election and where they can hire a trailer to take their lambs to the market and—'

'And you tell them,' suggested Gerald.

'I tell them,' agreed Mr MacTaggart complacently.

Gerald smiled. 'I've come to ask you something. I want a pair of thick grey stockings for stalking. Is there anyone in the village who could make them for me?'

'Katie will knit them for you,' replied Mr MacTaggart promptly. 'Katie MacTaggart, Colin's mother, is a good knitter and she will be glad of the money. Will I tell her or will you be seeing her yourself?'

Gerald replied that he would see her himself. He had been interested in Mac's account of the family and the stockings would give him an opportunity of meeting the young woman who was so anxious to make 'a nice home' for her boys.

'It is the wee cottage by the bridge,' said Mr MacTaggart. 'At one time it was the lodge. That was when the road to Tigh na Feidh was in good repair and the house was used by MacAslan's great-grandfather for his wild parties – Mad MacAslan they were calling him! Och, he was a great chief if you can believe all the stories,' added the innkeeper admiringly.

Gerald saw that Mr MacTaggart was about to embark upon the stories and, although he felt sure that they would be very interesting, he had no time to spare. He thanked Mr MacTaggart for his information and hastened away.

The cottage door was opened to him by a good-looking young woman with bright red hair – obviously Colin's mother!

There was no need for Gerald to introduce himself: she knew who he was of course (everybody in Ardfalloch knew who he was). She greeted him politely and invited him into her kitchen for a cup of tea. It was half past eleven and Gerald had just drunk a glass of ale at Mr MacTaggart's expense so he did not really want tea, but he was aware that if he wanted a chat with Mrs MacTaggart he would have to sit down at her kitchen table and drink a cup of tea and probably eat a scone.

The kitchen was small but beautifully clean and there was an array of gleaming pots and pans on the shelf above the old-fashioned iron stove. Mrs MacTaggart was genuinely pleased to see her visitor; Gerald got the impression that she was a little lonely and was ready for a chat. She spoke well, in a pleasant low voice without a trace of the local accent. He wondered who she was and where she had come from, but he did not need to 'wonder' long for she was quite willing to tell him.

Mrs MacTaggart's father was the owner of a flourishing bakery in Inverness. She had intended to take her training as a nurse but before she had finished her training she had met Neil MacTaggart who was a stalker in a big deer forest. They were both very young and her father was anxious for her to finish her training but she had not taken his advice. She married Neil and they went to live in a cottage on the hill. It was there that the three boys were born.

'We were very happy,' said Mrs MacTaggart with a little sigh. 'The boys grew up strong and healthy. They had freedom to go where they liked so they ran about like wild things and often went out with Neil and learnt about deer. Then Neil died and Mr Ferguson wanted the cottage for another stalker so of course we had to move. The boys and I went back to Inverness, to my father's house. It was kind of him to have us but it was not a success.'

'It was so different from what you were used to,' Gerald suggested.

'Quite different,' she agreed. 'The boys were not used to town life and they got into mischief. Colin was nineteen by that time – he is a good deal older than the others – and he could have got a post in Aberdeen, but that would have meant a break-up of the family, so I was glad when my husband's uncle found this post for him.'

'You wanted to make a nice home for your boys.'

'Yes, I wanted us to be together. It was what Neil would have wanted too, so I am hoping we can stay at Ardfalloch. Colin is a good boy and does his best but Mr MacGregor is difficult to please. That is the trouble, Mister Gerald.'

Tea was ready now and as she set it out on the table, Mrs MacTaggart went on talking. It was obvious that she was devoted to her boys. The two younger ones were at school in the village and were doing well . . . except that they preferred roaming over the hill to sitting in a class-room.

'Most boys do,' put in Gerald, smiling.

'Yes, but Sandy and wee Neil sometimes "play hookey",' replied their mother. 'Mr Black came and spoke to me about it . . . but what can I do? Sandy is the wildest. Sandy is as wild as heather and where Sandy goes wee Neil follows. Their father would have taken a strap to them but Colin just laughs and says it is good for them to be free. He says it is good to learn about deer when you are young. Sometimes they take a plaid and spend a night on the hill. At first I was worried but they are strong and healthy and they know how to look after themselves so it does them no harm.

They are very much stronger than they were when they were playing in the streets at Inverness.'

Gerald could well believe it.

'Are you enjoying the stalking?' asked Mrs MacTaggart. 'Colin was saying it is a very good forest with many fine stags. You killed a fine stag in the corrie on the shoulder of Ben Ghaoth.'

'How on earth did you hear about that?'

Mrs MacTaggart smiled. 'Colin saw you. Colin was disappointed that Mr MacGregor did not take him to see the sport so he put his glass in his pocket and went up the hill and watched from a distance. He saw you kill the ten-point stag and he saw the hornless stag get up from behind the rock and gallop up the bank. It passed quite near where Colin was lying and fled in terror. It was a huge beast, not elegant like a proper stag but coarse and ungainly. Colin says it ought to be killed before the rut.'

'You know a lot about stalking!'

She nodded. 'Neil used to talk to me – and now, Colin. I like to know what people are doing.'

They had finished tea by this time so Mrs MacTaggart fetched her work-bag, took out a long grey stocking and began to knit.

'That's what I want!' Gerald exclaimed. 'I want a pair of stockings just like that. Mr MacTaggart said you might have time to make them for me.'

'Indeed I will! Are you wanting them soon, Mister Gerald? I am making this pair for Colin and they are nearly finished. You can have them if you would like. Colin has several pairs so there is no hurry for him.'

Gerald did want them soon. In fact he wanted them to wear tomorrow if possible.

'You can have them today,' Mrs MacTaggart told him. 'The first stocking is finished and I have just to finish the foot of the second. If you can wait for half an hour you can take them with you. They will fit you nicely; you and Colin are just about the same size.'

Gerald agreed to wait. He had a feeling that Mrs Mac-Taggart would be glad of the money and, as he wanted the stockings, both were pleased with the bargain. He was amused to discover that the MacTaggart family were calling him 'Mister Gerald'. The innkeeper had done so – and, now, young Mrs MacTaggart! Perhaps they had meant to, or perhaps it had slipped out by mistake but Gerald found it pleasant. He thought it showed that they had accepted him as a friend.

13 In which Gerald relates a true story

The rain had stopped and the mist was clearing so Gerald went out and, leaning upon the parapet of the hump-backed bridge, watched the water swirling beneath its high arches. (It was a pleasant way of passing half an hour), but he had not been there for five minutes when he was joined by two boys. The bigger one had bright red hair, the smaller one was dark.

Gerald had had very little to do with children until he had met Alastair MacCallum and these two did not seem much older.

'Hullo, are you the MacTaggart boys?' he asked.

'Yes. I am Sandy and that is Neil,' replied the bigger one.

'Dinner is late,' said Neil with a sigh.

'So we were thinking we would talk to you,' explained Sandy.

Gerald took the point: it was his fault that dinner was late, so it was up to him to do something about it. 'What shall we talk about?' he asked, smiling at them.

'Neil is wanting to ask you something,' said Sandy.

'It was about Africa,' said Neil in a piping voice. 'It was in school. There is a big river in Africa with hipper-potter-musses. There was a picture of them in my book. I would like fine to see a hipper-potter-muss,' added Neil, looking up hopefully.

'I've seen them,' Gerald told him. 'They're ugly creatures – not like stags.'

'Did you shoot them, Mister Gerald?' asked Sandy eagerly.

'No, never.'

There was a short silence. It was obvious that the reply was disappointing.

'But I shot a lion,' added Gerald, offering the lion as second best.

'A lion?' breathed Sandy in awed tones. 'That's better than hipper-potter-musses. Lions are fierce.'

'Did the lion try to tear you to bits and eat you?' inquired Neil with interest.

'No, he didn't get the chance.'

'Tell us about it,' said Sandy eagerly. 'It's a story, isn't it? It's a true story. I like true stories best.'

'Yes, it's a true story,' said Gerald.

Two pairs of eyes were fixed upon him and he realised that he had let himself in for the story.

In Gerald's opinion the story was not very exciting but perhaps it would entertain the boys until their dinner was ready.

While Gerald was in South Africa a lion and a lioness had suddenly appeared and had wandered round outside the high iron fence which surrounded the diamond mine. They never came very near the fence but they disturbed everyone in the place with their roaring.

It was unusual to see lions at Koolbokie (nobody knew where they had come from) but it was reasonable to suppose that they had become too old to hunt and had wandered for miles looking for any sort of food that would stay the pangs of hunger. Lions in this condition are more dangerous than young active beasts as they are liable to become man-eaters if they can find no other food. The native 'boys' who worked in the mine knew this only too well and sent a deputation to the manager asking that the lions should be killed as soon as possible. Mr Proudfoot was aware that something must be done – already some of the 'boys' had fled in terror – so he borrowed a rifle from a friend in Johannesburg and asked Gerald to shoot them.

It was easy enough to say but not so easy to do. There was no sense in taking unnecessary risks – indeed it would have been foolish – for unless Gerald could be certain of killing the beasts outright they would be more dangerous than before. To add to his difficulties the borrowed rifle was an old weapon and a few practice shots with it proved it to be unreliable. This meant that he must get within easy reach of his prey.

Gerald remembered an old book, which had belonged to his father; it was *The Man-eaters of Tsavo* by Col. J. H. Patterson. He had not read it for years but it had fascinated him when he was a boy. Colonel Patterson had made traps for the lions but Gerald could not do this as he had neither the materials nor the labour. He did not lack advice, of course. When it was learned by his colleagues that he had been deputed to kill the lions Gerald received a great deal of advice as to how he should go about it but none of it seemed very sensible so he ignored it and made his own plans. He found a ruined hut on the hill above the mine and boarded up the windows, leaving an aperture from which to shoot. About thirty yards from the loophole he drove a strong stake into the ground and to this he tethered a goat. Then he took a thick rug, a flask of coffee and some sandwiches and settled himself in his hide-out.

The night was dark. There was no moon – and it was very quiet. Not a sound broke the silence. At first Gerald was all tensed up, straining his eyes and ears for signs of the lions, but towards morning he fell into an uneasy doze. He was awakened by a padding sound and realised that some beast was prowling stealthily round the hut . . .

Gerald paused here for a few moments. His audience, which

had been listening to every word in awed silence could contain itself no longer.

'It was the lion,' whispered Sandy.

'Yes, it was the lion. There was a space under the door. He stopped there and snuffled – and growled – I could hear him breathing heavily.'

'He had scented you?'

'Yes.'

'Were you frightened?'

'Yes,' replied Gerald frankly. As a matter of fact he was terrified. He realised he had been foolish. The hut was a crazy structure, burnt dry by the African sun. The beast had scented him and if it chose to attack him it could burst the door open with the greatest of ease. Gerald had seen lions before; he had seen them in menageries; he had seen them prowling about in Africa, but he had not realised they were so huge and fierce and strong. He had never been so close to a lion nor heard one snuffling nor smelt the sickening feral smell. He envisaged himself face to face with the monster, torn to pieces by a hungry lion with no hope of escape. Should he try to get out of the window? Would that give him more chance? Or should he aim his rifle at the door and hope to kill the beast with one bullet in a vital spot?

'Go on,' said Sandy breathlessly. 'The lion couldn't get in, could he?'

'Fortunately he didn't try.'

'Why didn't he?'

'The goat, which had been asleep, was wakened by the growling and tried to run away. Its chain rattled and it bleated. The lion heard it and was gone in a flash. It was still dark but dawn was breaking. There was just light enough for me to see his great tawny body bounding down the slope.'

'You shot him!' Sandy exclaimed.

'No, I waited. Dawn comes quickly when you're near the equator and I wanted to make sure of killing him. I waited until he had killed the goat and had begun to eat it. I waited until he turned sideways and then I shot him. I got him with both barrels one after the other just behind the shoulder . . .'

'Bang, bang!' shouted Neil, jumping up and down in glee.

'Did you kill him?' asked Sandy.

'I wasn't sure. He rolled over and over several times. I reloaded quickly and let him have another. The sun was rising and it was getting lighter every moment. Then, suddenly, about a dozen native boys appeared on the scene. They rushed down from a pile of rocks where they had been hiding and set about the beast's carcase, slashing it with knives and bashing it with crowbars and shouting like maniacs.'

'Why did they?'

'They were pleased that it was dead . . . but I was furious with them. I was waiting for the lioness – I was sure she was somewhere about – and I wanted to bag her too. I thought the noise would frighten her away and I should have to spend another night waiting for her to come . . . but it didn't frighten her away. She came from the opposite direction, slinking along and taking cover where possible. She was long and lean and tawny – the same colour as the withered grass – so it wasn't easy to see her. I yelled to the boys to look out but they were making such a racket that they didn't hear me and it wasn't until she was almost on them that they realised their danger and fled. They scattered and fled in all directions. It would have been funny if it hadn't been so dangerous.'

'Did she go after them?'

'She hesitated. She couldn't make up her mind whether to go after them or not. She was about a hundred yards

from the hut and if I had had a decent rifle I could have
got her quite easily, but I hadn't so I couldn't be certain
of killing her outright. If I had wounded her she would have
been even more dangerous.'

Gerald paused again. He remembered that moment as if
it were yesterday . . . that moment and the awful decision he
had been obliged to make!

'Go on, Mister Gerald!' urged Sandy.

'I had just made up my mind to risk it, and was taking
careful aim when the beast saw the remains of the goat
– or perhaps she smelt the blood. She let out a roar and, leaping up the slope, started on her meal. It was easy to see that
the brute was ravenously hungry; she tore and crunched
and snuffled and snorted. She was so hungry that she paid
no attention to the carcass of her mate which was lying only
a few yards away. I waited until she was in a good position
and then I killed her.'

'With one shot?'

'I gave her two, just to make certain, but there was no
need. She was a sitting target: I couldn't have missed her.'

There was a short silence. Then the questions began: the
questions were intelligent and searching – these boys knew
a good deal about shooting – but Gerald had told his tale.

'Look!' he said. 'There's your mother waving to you.
Your dinner is ready.'

'Just one question!' cried Sandy, clinging to his arm. 'Just
one – please, Mister Gerald! Did you have the heads
mounted like gentlemen do when they kill a stag?'

'No, I didn't,' Gerald replied. 'They were old beasts, lean
and mangy, and by the time the native boys had bashed
them about there wasn't much left of them . . . and anyhow
I didn't want them. I didn't want to remember what I had
done.'

'Why?' asked Sandy in surprise. 'Were you not proud?'

Gerald found it difficult to explain. He had not been proud of his achievement, nor had he been ashamed. It was just a job that he had had to do and he had done it. He was very tired so he had returned to his bungalow and had got into bed and gone to sleep. He had slept for hours (so deeply that the screams and yells of jubilation had not disturbed him) and by the time he wakened the excitement was over. Some of his friends had tried to congratulate him but he had accepted their congratulations ungraciously. He remembered saying, 'For goodness' sake don't talk about it! It was horrible. If any more lions come to Koolbokie someone else can kill them. I just want to forget about the brutes.'

And the odd thing was that he had – almost – forgotten about the brutes. He had mentioned the lions to Mac, of course, but that was merely 'by the way'. It was not until he had started to tell his story to the MacTaggarts that it had come back into his head with all its grisly details!

Gerald was sorry now that he had told them, for he realised that his simple tale had made him a hero in their eyes and he had no desire to be a hero!

Sandy was still clinging to his arm. 'Mister Gerald,' he was saying. 'Mister Gerald, listen! Lions are brave. If a lion is wounded he comes for you but a stag runs away.'

'They're made differently. They have different instincts.'

'A stag eats grass and a lion eats people.'

'Not always, Sandy. It's only when lions are old and can't catch antelopes and zebras that they may become man-eaters.'

'If a lion was coming to Ard na Feidh he would kill a stag and eat it.'

'A lion couldn't come here. Lions live in Africa so—'

'If he escaped from a circus he could come here.'

'There was a circus at Kincraig,' put in Neil. 'Sandy and me were creeping under the tent and we were seeing the lion in his cage. He was sleeping . . . but he woke up when the man came along with a bit of meat on the end of a stick and pushed it into his cage.'

'It was bloody,' said Sandy.

'There!' cried Neil, jumping up and down like a jack-in-the-box. 'There! You said it! Mother said she would be putting soap in your mouth if you were saying it again!'

'I was not saying it like a swear,' replied Sandy in a dignified manner. 'I was not, was I, Mister Gerald?'

Gerald was trying to disguise his chuckles by a fit of coughing so he was unable to reply.

'Mister Gerald,' said Neil. 'If a lion was very hungry would he be eating grass – like a stag?'

'No,' replied Gerald. 'His stomach isn't meant to digest grass any more than yours is. Look, your mother is beckoning to you! We had better go back to the cottage.'

He began to walk back to the cottage with the two boys (who were surprisingly heavy) clinging to his arms.

Mrs MacTaggart saw them coming and rushed out: 'Sandy! Neil!' she cried. 'What a way to behave! What are you thinking of? Come here at once! Oh, Mister Gerald, I am sorry they have been bothering you! I had no idea—'

'They haven't been bothering me,' replied Gerald, smiling. 'They're very amusing and intelligent. We've been talking about lions.'

'It *is* kind of you,' declared Mrs MacTaggart. She added, 'They have no father, you see.'

Gerald was very thoughtful as he walked back to Tigh na Feidh with the stockings in his pocket: there had been tears in Mrs MacTaggart's eyes.

14 Which describes a picnic by the river

The weather was better that week so Gerald and Oliver went out nearly every day with Malcolm. Gerald killed a switch – it was an old, done beast and Malcolm was glad to see it killed.

Oliver killed two nice young stags with reasonably good heads and was pleased with his performance, but he had set his heart upon a 'Royal'. He confided to Gerald that he intended to have the head stuffed and mounted to give to his mother for Christmas. Needless to say Lucius Cottar had the finest Royal that Oliver had ever seen. It was in the hall of his house at Ascot and was much admired by all his sporting friends.

At a matter of fact Oliver Stoddart was surprisingly pleasant. He was the sort of young man who is pleasant and agreeable when he gets exactly what he wants – and Oliver was getting what he wanted. The weather was fine, he was getting good sport and haunches of venison to send to all his friends.

He disliked Gerald Burleigh Brown, and was jealous of the man's friendship with the MacAslans, but he was clever enough to realise that any display of animosity would do him no good. Oliver had a feeling that there was something mysterious about the man : he received very few letters; he rarely wrote letters and he had refused Mac's offer of venison to despatch to friends. In addition to these peculiarities he seldom spoke about himself. That was odd, thought Oliver, who was never happier than when he was holding forth about his own doings.

Oliver had written to two friends who had an orange farm in South Africa asking them to find out anything they could about Gerald Burleigh Brown and was awaiting their reply.

Mac was busy that week. He had received instructions from his father about Ardfalloch House. A new bathroom was being installed and the kitchen premises were being painted and redecorated – nothing had been done to them for years – so he went down to the Big House nearly every day to see that the work was being carried out satisfactorily. This meant that he was unable to stalk with his guests but Mac was unselfish and as long as his guests were happy, and were getting good sport, he was content and cheerful.

Colin MacTaggart was not so cheerful. He had been out twice with 'Mister MacGregor' and the two gentlemen but 'Mister MacGregor' gave him no chance to show his mettle, and he was beginning to wonder if he would be kept on at Ard na Feidh and, if not, what he should do. If he were dismissed the family would have to move from the cottage to make room for another man. The responsibilities of his family weighed heavily upon his young shoulders.

A few days after this Mac received an invitation from Mr Ross of Glen Veigh to go over for a grouse drive and bring a friend. The moors at Glen Veigh were exceedingly good, and famous for the size of their bag, so an invitation to shoot there was very much sought-after.

'You must come, Gerald!' cried Mac, waving a letter in Gerald's face. 'You said you had never shot grouse so it will be a new experience for you.'

Oliver was annoyed. The last time he had been here the invitation had come and he had gone with MacAslan – and had enjoyed his day immensely – this time he was to be left at home!

Gerald smiled. 'No, Mac,' he said. 'You had better take Stoddart.'

'Nonsense!' cried Mac. 'Oliver won't mind. He's shot grouse hundreds of times. You don't mind, do you, Oliver?'

'No, of course not,' replied Oliver in grudging tones. 'The only thing is Mr Ross is keen on a good bag and if Burleigh Brown hasn't had any experience of grouse-shooting . . .'

'That's right,' agreed Gerald. 'Stoddart will do you more credit. He's the man to take.'

'But I want you to come,' Mac expostulated. 'I want you to meet Mr Ross. You'd like him!'

Gerald shook his head. 'I'm not much good with a gun. Honestly, Mac, you had better take Stoddart.'

Mac was annoyed – and disappointed. It was Gerald he wanted to take. Possibly Gerald would not kill as many birds as Oliver but he was a much more interesting personality (Gerald was a friend to be proud of whereas poor old Oliver was really becoming rather a bore).

'Oh, all right,' said Mac with manifest reluctance.

Mr Ross had chosen a Saturday for his Big Shoot because he was able to recruit the schoolchildren to augment his staff of beaters. He would have got them anyway, whatever day he had chosen (not only did the children prefer a day on the moors to a day in the class-room but the money they earned was useful to their parents) but Mr Ross liked to keep on good terms with his neighbours and had no desire to fall foul of Mr Black.

The Land-Rover had been brought to Tigh na Feidh on Friday so on Saturday morning Mac and Oliver started out immediately after breakfast, accompanied by Malcolm and Colin, to act as loaders. Gerald and the two girls watched them depart with their guns and cartridges and other impedimenta, including a large cumbersome shooting-stick which could be used as an umbrella. This belonged to Oliver, of course. It had been given to him by his friend, Lucius Cottar.

'You should have gone,' said Phil, when the Land-Rover had bumped off down the rutty road. 'You would have enjoyed it, Gerald. Why should Oliver always get his own way?'

Gerald smiled. 'Because it's so much more pleasant for everybody when he does.'

'Yes,' agreed Phil. 'There's that, of course, but it's so terribly bad for him.'

'Mac was disappointed,' said Donny with a sigh.

There was a lot left unsaid in the short conversation but there was no need to say more. The three were in complete accord.

'What shall we do?' asked Phil. 'You're in for a dull day, Gerald. Would you like to take lunch and go for a picnic?'

'Yes, that's a marvellous idea!' Gerald exclaimed.

The girls went to the kitchen to fill Thermos flasks and make sandwiches and in a very short time the three friends were starting out for their picnic.

'I'm going to take you in the other direction today,' said Phil. 'We'll go up the valley towards Achnaluig.'

'I don't mind where we go,' replied Gerald. 'This is one of the most beautiful places I've ever seen . . . and it's so peaceful! Time seems to stand still.'

'I'm glad you're happy here,' said Phil simply. 'You'll come again next year, won't you?'

'If I can,' said Gerald. 'It all depends on when I get my holiday. You know that, of course.' He hesitated and then added, 'There's no other place in the world I would rather go to.'

Donny said nothing. She walked along beside them like a little shadow. She seemed to be lost in dreams.

It was a glorious day: the sun shone with golden brilliance; the sky was pale blue; a few fleecy clouds hovered over the hills.

They had reached the river by this time: the place where the little Ard na Feidh burn joined the river in a long silver cascade. Here the river ran through a wood of birch trees; it ran quickly, twisting this way and that way, prattling cheerfully in its stony bed. The birches had just begun to turn colour and amongst the green foliage a splash of gold showed where the frost had touched a branch and passed on. Away to the north the valley was spread before them, green and fertile, behind them the hills rose steeply, their rocky summits cutting a jagged line against the sky.

Phil loved this spot. It was the place she had chosen for their picnic lunch. She sank down, softly as a snowflake upon the mossy turf and looked up at Gerald with her lovely smile.

'Isn't this a beautiful place for a picnic?' said Phil.

If she had expected raptures she was disappointed.

Gerald sat down beside her. He said, 'Oh Phil, I want to talk to you.'

'But you talk to me every day!'

'Not alone. I never see you alone – not for a moment. I haven't seen you alone since that first afternoon when you showed me my room and told me about the forest. There's always someone there: Stoddart, writing letters, or Mac reading a book, or Donny sewing – or something.'

'Where's Donny?' Phil exclaimed, looking round.

'She just wandered away.'

'Perhaps she's lost!'

'No,' said Gerald. 'I expect Donny knew I wanted to talk to you . . . and just . . . wandered away.'

'We had better look for her!'

'There's no need to look for her.'

'But Gerald, perhaps she has got lost—'

'Donny isn't silly.'

'No, she isn't,' agreed Phil smiling. 'Donny is quite clever in her own way. You like her, don't you?'

'Of course I like her. I'd like anyone you were fond of. But I don't want to talk about Donny, I want to talk about us. Oh, Phil, please listen—'

'We're friends, aren't we?' she interrupted breathlessly. 'We're friends, Gerald. Mac likes you awfully much. It's so good for Mac to have a friend like you. Mac is a bit wild sometimes – he's just a boy really – and some of his friends are – are rather queer. I mean they have queer ideas about things. For instance, Mac refuses to speak the Gaelic – he "had the Gaelic" when he was little so he could soon rub it up and it would be so useful to be able to speak to the people here in their very own language. They like it, you know. I wish you would persuade him, Gerald. Mac admires you so much that I'm sure he would listen to you.'

'I'm sure he wouldn't! We were talking about it the other day and he told me what he thought about the Gaelic. His views were very definite and he isn't likely to change them . . . but Phil, need we talk about Mac and his views? I want to talk about us – about you and me. I want to tell you about my feelings. There's nobody like you, Phil. Nobody in the whole wide world. I thought that the first time I saw you – and I shall always feel the same. Please say you like me just a little—'

'Of course I like you,' interrupted Phil. 'I've just been telling you that I want you as a friend. I wouldn't want you as a friend if I didn't like you.'

Gerald gave it up. He said, 'I shall have to go back to Glasgow tomorrow.'

'Oh Gerald, why?'

'It's my work. There's a lot to do.'

'But I thought you liked being here! I thought you were

having your holiday! I know you don't get on very well
with Oliver but you mustn't mind what he says . . .'

'I don't mind what he says,' muttered Gerald.

'. . . and I expect he'll be going away soon,' added Phil.

Gerald was silent. Another man might have made a more
determined effort but Gerald was too sensitive to press his
case. It was obvious that Phil did not want to listen : she had
put up a barrier and had retreated behind it.

'We had better have lunch,' said Phil. She rose as she
spoke and shouted for Donny to come.

Donny had walked up the hill by a little path which wound
its way through the birchwood. She came down slowly,
hoping to find two happy people sitting together on the
river bank. Perhaps they would be holding each other's
hands! Perhaps they would have something very interesting
to tell her! But although they had had half an hour (which
ought to have been enough) it was apparent that something
had gone wrong. Gerald was too silent and Phil too
talkative.

Donny was a gentle creature so it was strange that she
should have felt so angry with her friends – so angry that
she would have liked to shake them! She could say nothing. She could do nothing. Later, perhaps, when she and
Phil were alone (when they were wandering in and out of
each other's rooms getting ready for bed) Phil might tell her
about it . . . but she wouldn't ask of course.

15 Is conversational

Mac and Oliver returned from Glen Veigh in time for the evening meal. They were full of their day's sport: it had been a big party and they had made a record bag. The grouse-moors at Glen Veigh were well preserved and Mr Ross chose his guns with discrimination so it was considered an honour to be asked to shoot at Glen Veigh. Mac and Oliver were quite pleased with themselves, especially Oliver, who talked all through the meal about what he had done, and about his fellow guests and what they had said. According to Oliver they had all been very complimentary about the performance of Oliver Stoddart.

The new Chief Constable of the County of Northshire had been there: one Major Kane, a retired regular who had seen service in the Second War. Mac had talked to him at lunch and liked him immensely. Oliver thought him too lighthearted – too facetious. A Chief Constable ought to be dignified, complained Oliver. There was no dignity about the man.

'What nonsense!' cried Mac. 'Look at his war record! He was all through the campaign in France and Germany. He was awarded the M.C. at the crossing of the Rhine! Mr Ross said he ought to have got the V.C.'

'That's easily said,' declared Oliver. 'Hundreds of men ought to have got the V.C. in their own estimation.'

'It wasn't his "own estimation",' Mac retorted. His Colonel put him up for it. Mr Ross told me. Anyway I liked Major Kane. There's no red-tape about him. He'll do what he thinks right – and if his superiors think he's done wrong they can sack him. That's what he said.'

'What an extraordinary thing to say!'

'It isn't extraordinary,' Mac declared. 'It's the right thing. He has been given a responsible position and he intends to exert his authority—'

'He intends to throw his weight about, I suppose?'

'That's right!' exclaimed Mac heatedly. 'There are far too many yes-men in responsible positions. There are far too many men who are so strangled with red-tape that they can't open their mouths. Major Kane isn't afraid of anybody. If I were in a hole I'd go straight to Major Kane . . .'

The argument continued, becoming more and more heated every minute, so the combatants were much too excited to notice that their three companions were unusually silent and abstracted.

Gerald had been happy at Tigh na Feidh. He had been almost sure that Phil was fond of him for, although he had had no opportunity of speaking to her in private, she had accepted his little attentions and smiled at him so sweetly. Perhaps it had been wishful thinking but – yes – he had been certain she was fond of him. He loved her so dearly that he could not believe his love was not returned. But today she had made it clear that she wanted him as a friend: a friend for herself and for Mac.

Phil was no 'flirt'. She was absolutely open and natural. She was as honest as the day. She had refused to listen; she had put up a barrier and he could not get near her any more. What should he do? Was it any good trying to break down the barrier? Wouldn't it be better to go back to Glasgow and settle down to work? There was plenty to do there. He could work until he was too tired to think.

They had finished the meal by this time so they moved to

the big chairs and the sofa which were grouped round the fire.

The movement broke up the argument and gave Gerald his chance. He said quietly, 'Mac, I'm afraid I shall have to go back to Glasgow sooner than I intended.'

'What!' cried Mac in dismay. 'You've only been here ten days! I thought you had got three weeks' holiday! Gerald, you can't mean it! Have you had a letter from Sir Walter?'

'No, but there's a lot to do. I think I had better go tomorrow.'

'You can't,' declared Mac. 'Tomorrow is Sunday. Please stay, Gerald. I know you've had a dull day but we'll have a splendid day on Monday and another on Tuesday. The weather is clearing – Malcolm says so. Do stay for a few days longer . . . unless you're bored, of course.'

'Of course I'm not bored! I've enjoyed myself immensely. It's just that I feel I ought to go back.'

Mac did not understand it at all (how could he?) and he continued to press his friend to stay. He was so upset about it that Gerald felt obliged to agree.

'But I must go back on Wednesday,' said Gerald firmly. That meant two more days at Tigh na Feidh – two more days of seeing Phil and not being able to get near her! – but Gerald comforted himself by the reflection that it would be easy enough to avoid seeing her except at mealtimes when the others would be there.

On Sunday Mac and Phil and Donny went off to church and Oliver settled down to write letters. (Oliver received an immense number of letters and spent hours answering them.) So Gerald put a slice of bread and cheese in his pocket and set off by himself for a walk. It was a dull cold day with an occasional shower, but Gerald found walking pleasant. He strode along manfully over the hills. By this time he knew most of the forest quite well. The only parts he did not know were the northern slopes, which were avoided by the deer, so Gerald went that way and scrambled about amongst the rocks and the fading heather. There were bogs here and a few stunted trees: rowans with twisted branches. It was a bleak sort of place – Gerald was not really surprised that the deer avoided it – but he found a sheltered nook and sat down to have his bread and cheese. Then he drank some water from a neighbouring burn and walked home to Tigh na Feidh.

He felt better now. The exercise in the fresh air had cleared his head and he decided to have a talk with Mac. Mac was the only person in the house with whom he could have a private conversation without fear of interruption. He could knock on Mac's door whenever he felt inclined and go in and talk to him while he was dressing. (He could have done the same to Oliver Stoddart, of course, but as he never wanted a private conversation with Stoddart, the idea had never crossed his mind.)

16   Is confidential

It was nearly time for supper when Gerald returned from his walk and as he went upstairs he heard Mac moving about in his room across the landing so he tapped on the door and went in.

'Hullo, where have you been?' asked Mac.

Gerald told him.

'It's queer, isn't it?' said Mac. 'Something a bit uncanny about it! As a matter of fact there's quite good feeding in places but the deer avoid it.'

'I don't wonder,' said Gerald. He hesitated and then added, 'I got rather a fright. I nearly got stuck in a bog . . . just realised in time that I was sinking and managed to back out.'

'The bogs up there aren't really dangerous,' Mac told him. 'There's so much rock, you see. You wouldn't have sunk very far – just over your ankles. If the bogs were really dangerous we should have to put fences round them. See?'

'Yes, I see.'

There was a short silence. Mac was changing his socks.

'Look here, Mac,' said Gerald. 'I don't want you to think I haven't enjoyed being here. It's a lovely place . . .'

'Well, why are you thinking of going away? Is it because of Oliver? He has become an awful bore but he doesn't mean to be nasty and I think he has had an invitation from Lucius Cottar.'

'Oh, has he?'

'And another thing,' Mac continued. 'I *do* want you to

meet Dad. I don't know when he's coming but he won't stay in Edinburgh much longer – if I know anything about him. You'd like to meet him, wouldn't you?'

'Yes, of course,' said Gerald. This was perfectly true. Gerald had heard so much about MacAslan that he would have liked to see him in the flesh.

'Do stay a bit longer,' said Mac looking up and smiling boyishly. 'Please stay a bit longer, Gerald.'

Gerald hesitated. He liked Mac so much that it was difficult to refuse.

'You will!' cried Mac. 'That's lovely. You'll stay until the end of the week, won't you? By that time Oliver will have gone – and perhaps Dad will have come – and we shall all be much more comfortable.'

'The only thing is—'

'Phil thinks he will come quite soon,' Mac interrupted. 'Phil thinks he's getting restive . . . and Phil knows a lot about Dad. There's a special sort of relationship between them. I mean they have scarcely ever been parted. Phil went to school for one term but she absolutely refused to go back: they were both so miserable that they couldn't bear it. I don't know what will happen to Dad when Phil gets married,' added Mac, frowning thoughtfully.

'Is she . . . thinking of getting married?' asked Gerald.

'She's sort of engaged.'

'What do you mean by "sort of"?'

'Well, it's been an understood thing since she and Simon were kids that some day, when they were older, they would marry each other. They weren't "engaged" exactly. I mean as far as I know Simon didn't give her a ring . . . but they used to write to each other regularly. I don't know whether they still write to each other.'

'I see,' said Gerald.

'It's difficult,' Mac continued. 'Phil wouldn't leave Dad stranded of course – and he would be absolutely stranded without her. She thought at one time that he might marry again. She had a plan that he might marry Miss Finlay of Cluan (they've been friends for years and years so Phil thought it would be nice for them) but the plan didn't come off. As a matter of fact I don't believe Dad wants to marry anybody. He's perfectly happy with Phil.'

'I see,' repeated Gerald.

'And another thing,' continued Mac. 'Another thing is that Phil loves Ardfalloch. I don't believe she really wants to leave Ardfalloch and go and live in the south of England. It's all rather vague.'

'Who is Simon?' Gerald asked.

'Simon Wentworth. He's a baronet with a big estate and a lot of money. He's at Cambridge just now. I don't know what he's supposed to be doing there . . . except playing cricket and acting in plays and having a jolly good time.'

'I see,' said Gerald. He added, 'But, Mac, if they were in love with each other—'

'Oh, I know! If they were in love they'd want to get married, I suppose. I mean if people are in love they're sort of potty, aren't they? I've never been potty about a girl but I've seen it happen to quite sensible chaps,' added Mac.

'I'm "potty" about a girl,' admitted Gerald with a rueful smile. 'I never thought it would happen to me – but it has.'

'Well, why don't you marry her?'

'It's Phil.'

'Phil?' echoed Phil's brother incredulously.

'That's why I asked you—'

'Good Lord! How amazing! You mean you want to marry Phil?'

'Yes.'

'How amazing!' repeated Mac, gazing at his friend in blank astonishment. He added hastily, 'It would be very nice, of course.'

'Not as "nice" as a wealthy baronet with a big estate.'

'It would be "nicer",' declared Mac. 'I mean you and I are pals, aren't we?'

'Yes.'

'And, between you and me,' said Mac thoughtfully. 'In strict confidence, of course, I don't believe Phil would be happy at Limbourne.'

'Why not?'

'It's too grand. Everything at Limbourne is terribly grand. If you want a cup of tea you can't pop into the kitchen and make it for yourself. You ring for the butler and he brings it on a silver tray. You're almost afraid to sit down in a chair in case you crush the cushions.'

Gerald was smiling now: he couldn't help it.

'It's true,' declared Mac. 'I stayed there once for the week-end, so I know. When I got up the footman came in and beat up the cushions. I'm not very tidy. Phil isn't very tidy either. We're apt to leave things lying about but you can't do that at Limbourne. The footman follows you and picks them up and puts them away. He comes into your bedroom and tidies it up. It made me feel an awful fool, really. The garden is terribly tidy. The paths have neatly cut edges and the rose bushes are pruned to within an inch of their lives . . . there isn't a weed to be seen! You know the sort of thing, don't you?'

'Yes,' said Gerald.

'The country is tame,' continued Mac. 'There are no hills . . . well, there *is* a hill, but it's tame.'

'A tame hill?'

Mac nodded. 'I suppose it must have been wild at one time, but they've brushed and combed it and tied a ribbon round its neck.'

'Paths?' suggested Gerald.

'Yes, gravelled paths and neat steps with wooden banisters and seats where you can sit down and admire the view. It's a pretty view,' admitted Mac. 'There are farms and green meadows with cows in them and there's a stream moving along slowly and sleepily . . . and on Sundays you can see men sitting on the banks watching a cork bobbing about in the water. If the cork disappears they pull in their line and there's a fish on the hook. That's what they call fishing,' added Mac, not so much scornfully as compassionately.

'And another thing,' continued Mac very thoughtfully indeed. 'Another thing is that if Phil married Simon she would be absorbed into the Wentworth family and wouldn't belong to us any more. I can't explain properly but I know what I mean.'

Gerald thought he had explained the matter pretty well.

'I wouldn't want to absorb Phil,' said Gerald gravely. 'If Phil were to marry me we should have to live in Glasgow because of my job, but Ardfalloch means a lot to her. I'd want her to come here often. I'd want her to have the best of both worlds, Mac.'

'Yes,' agreed Mac. 'Yes, you understand Phil . . . but there's still Dad, of course. He's the real snag.'

Gerald sighed. He saw that this was true: MacAslan was the real snag. He had not seen the man of course but you could not spend a week at Ardfalloch without realising that everybody in the place worshipped the ground he trod on . . . including his son and daughter. Mac was forever moaning and wishing his father were here . . . and, although Phil did not moan so much, her face when she spoke of him showed her feelings all too clearly . . . and when she received his letters she seized them and gloated over them (as a mother might gloat over the letters of a beloved child).

So that was that, thought Gerald. He must just grin and bear it. He must 'make do' with Phil's friendship and put the nearer and dearer relationship out of his head.

'I wish Dad were here,' said Mac, breaking a short silence. 'There's something special I want to ask him about.

It's about the MacTaggarts. Malcolm was at me again today about Colin. He keeps on saying Colin will never be any good on the hill – but he hasn't really given the boy a chance.'

'They're good people,' declared Gerald, putting in a word for his friends.

'I know,' Mac agreed. 'The fact is everybody at Ardfalloch is getting old. We need young people here and it isn't easy to find young people who are willing to settle down in the country.'

'The MacTaggarts would.'

'Yes, the MacTaggarts would. Young Mrs MacTaggart was in church this morning; she spoke to me afterwards and said they liked being here. She would be willing to come to Ardfalloch House and help Janet if we wanted her. That would be a godsend! Janet must be over eighty, so she really isn't fit for work. The MacTaggart boys would be useful too; they could be pony-boys when they're a bit older. What do you think about it, Gerald?'

'I think they're all good value.'

'Malcolm is the trouble,' said Mac, frowning thoughtfully.

'Why?' asked Gerald. 'Why has he got his knife into Colin?'

'Oh, because of his cousin. He wanted us to engage his cousin, Fergus MacGregor, but Fergus is an experienced stalker and we can't afford to have two experienced stalkers at Ard na Feidh. Besides, Fergus is as old as Malcolm. We want somebody young. We want a man who will settle down and learn all about the forest so that he can take over when Malcolm retires.'

Gerald nodded. 'It's jealousy, of course. What are you going to do about it?'

'I can't do much,' replied Mac, with a sigh. 'The only person who can cope with Malcolm is Dad.'

'MacAslan is always right,' murmured Gerald.

'What's that?'

'Malcolm said it,' Gerald replied. 'I'm just quoting, that's all. If you want my advice you'll write to your father and explain the whole matter – just as you've explained it to me.'

'Yes,' agreed Mac. 'Yes, that's what to do. You'll help me to write the letter, won't you? I'm not very good at explaining things, especially on paper. If only Dad were here we could talk it over properly. That would be much easier, of course. Meantime I've arranged to take Colin tomorrow morning and go after the hummel. I want to see for myself what sort of stuff Colin is made of.'

'I expect Colin is pleased,' suggested Gerald.

'Yes, he seemed very pleased,' replied Mac.

17   In which Colin lays his plans

Colin had been very pleased indeed when he heard that he was to go out on Monday morning and stalk the hummel. He was determined to do his best and to show young MacAslan that he was worth his salt. To this end he requisitioned the services of his two young brothers and the three of them spent the whole of Sunday on the hills searching for the big hornless stag. By nightfall they had spotted the creature down near the river beyond the Black Pass. It was a favourite haunt of the hinds. There were hinds there now and the hummel was interested in them; he was moving about restlessly on the outskirts of the herd.

Colin knew that at any moment he might start chasing them . . . and a stag that is chasing hinds moves far and fast. This meant that Sandy and Neil must spend the night on the hill: the beast would not move far in the darkness and the boys would be here at dawn to see which way he went. Colin was not going to lose the beast now, after all the trouble they had had in finding him!

The boys were delighted; they had spent nights on the hill before and had enjoyed the experience. It would be even better fun tonight for Colin had given them a responsible task which made them feel important.

Colin left them his plaid and went home to tell his mother what had happened.

'I am hoping I will do well tomorrow,' said Colin as he sat down to have his supper.

'You will do well, Colin,' said Mrs MacTaggart encouragingly. She was aware that Colin was to be on trial tomorrow and was anxious that he should do well. She gave him a good supper and sent him to bed early so that he should be strong and fresh for the day's sport.

Meanwhile the boys found a sheltered cranny between two boulders, wrapped themselves in Colin's plaid, curled up together like a couple of puppies and went to sleep.

The rising sun woke them and they saw the hinds moving up the valley towards Ben Ghaoth. The hornless beast was pursuing them. Sometimes he galloped after them and they fled like the wind; sometimes he dropped to a walk and the hinds stopped and turned their graceful heads to look back.

'They are not wanting that one,' said Sandy slyly.

'He is ugly,' Neil agreed.

The sun rose higher above the mountains; its beams crept down the hill into the valley. It was shining directly into the boys' eyes so they shaded their eyes with their grubby little paws and watched patiently to see what would happen. After a little while a twelve-pointer stag came over the ridge at the upper end of the valley. He stood on the crest of the hill in the sunshine and stretched his neck as though he were about to roar . . . but no sound came.

The boys were high up on the hill, hidden in the deep heather, and the scene was spread before their eyes like a picture in a book.

'It is nice,' said wee Neil. 'Nicer than school, Sandy. Will he roar, do you think?'

'The Day of Roaring has not come,' Sandy replied.

'But there are times when they will be roaring before the Day. Look, Sandy, he is trying again!'

The stag stretched his neck out three times and at last the roar came. It was a tentative sort of roar (by no means the full throated 'Ha, ha!' that shakes the mountains when the rut is at its height) but, for all that, it was exciting.

'Will they be fighting, these two?' asked Neil.

'They will not,' replied Sandy scornfully. 'They will not

be fighting. A stag would not be fighting with a hornless beast.'

The hinds had stopped on beholding the twelve-pointer but when he roared they turned suddenly and with one accord set off up the hill. They passed within a hundred yards of the boys' hiding-place but the wind was in their nostrils so they were unaware that anyone was watching. There were about twenty hinds, lithe and graceful, reddish brown in colour, and about half that number of biggish calves. The whole party disappeared over the crest of the hill and was gone in a flash.

The two stags, horned and hornless, remained behind. They eyed each other for a few minutes. Then the twelve-pointer threw up his heels and went after the hinds. The hummel began to graze.

'That is fine,' said Sandy with a sigh of relief. 'Listen, Neil, you will go down to the cottage and tell Colin that he is still here.'

18 Which describes the stalking of the hummel

Gerald awoke to hear the stag roaring. He had not heard the sound before but Mac had told him it was a prelude to 'the rut'. (As a matter of fact Gerald was a little disappointed; he had been told that the roaring of a stag was like that of a lion and this roar was feeble in comparison.)

A few moments later Mac tapped on his door and came in.

'Did you hear it?' he asked eagerly. 'It wasn't a proper "roar" of course, it was just a sort of rehearsal. You should hear them in October when the rut is in full swing – it's grand! I like when the rut starts. It makes stalking more difficult but that's half the fun. You must get another stag today, Gerald.'

'I don't want to kill another.'

'What do you mean?' asked Mac. 'You're going out with Malcolm and Oliver this morning. It's all arranged—'

'I told you,' Gerald interrupted. 'I told you I would kill one fine stag (if I could) because you and your father wanted me to do it, but I don't want to kill another. We agreed that I was a freak.' He smiled and added, 'Besides, I wouldn't get a chance, would I?'

'What do you mean? Malcolm has seen a Royal on the other side of Ben Ghaoth. It will be a pretty stiff climb but you don't mind that, do you?'

'Stoddart will kill the Royal if we happen to see him.'

'Oliver has killed lots of stags—'

'But he has set his heart on the Royal.'

'Gerald, listen—'

'Don't worry,' said Gerald, smiling. 'Friend Oliver Stoddart is quite determined to have the Royal. "He won't be happy till he gets it"! He intends to hang the head on the wall of his mother's dining-room in Glasgow. He told me so himself. I'd rather come with you, if you'll have me.'

'Of course I'd love to have you, but you'd have better sport with the others,' declared Mac. He added, 'I'm taking Colin and going after the hummel.'

'Yes, I know. I'd like to see you bag the hummel. He's so big and ugly, isn't he?'

They had seen the hummel twice since their first glimpse of him in the corrie but so far he had managed to elude them. The beast seemed to have an uncanny knowledge of the approach of danger; he would graze quietly until his enemies were almost within shooting distance of him and then make off at a clumsy gallop startling every stag in the neighbourhood.

'Yes, he's huge,' agreed Mac with a sigh. He added, 'Well, just do as you like, Gerald. If I'd known you were so keen to see the end of the hummel I'd have taken Malcolm – we don't know what Colin can do – but we can't change it now. I arranged with him on Saturday that he was to meet me at the stepping-stones at the usual time.'

It began to rain as Gerald and Mac started off to meet Colin so Gerald stopped to put on his rainproof coat (there was no sense in getting wet if it could be avoided). Colin was waiting for them with the boy and the second pony. He greeted the two gentlemen politely and began to lead the way up the road to the Black Pass.

'Here, wait a moment, Colin!' said Mac. 'We're not going that way.' He had decided to cross the burn and climb the hill, for it was there that they had last seen the hummel and from there they could get a good view of the tops and might be able to pick out their quarry with a telescope.

'We will be going through the Black Pass,' said Colin, smiling ingratiatingly.

'Through the Pass! But why? We shan't be able to see anything from there,' objected Mac.

'It will be the best thing,' Colin assured him. 'We shall be seeing the hornless stag from the Pass.'

'How do you know?'

Colin gazed at the hills for inspiration. 'It is just an idea I am having,' he declared.

'Have you seen him?'

'How would I be seeing him?' asked Colin in surprise.

Mac frowned thoughtfully: he had to make up his mind what to do. He knew that the stags preferred the high ground but, on the other hand, Colin might be right. Colin was obviously keen to do his best so it was unlikely that he would insist on dragging them up to the Pass unless he had reason to believe that the hummel was in that direction. Why couldn't the man say definitely whether or not he had seen the beast? The answer was that these people never did answer questions definitely, thought Mac in exasperation. MacAslan could have spoken to the man in Gaelic and got it out of him – but Mac could not. Mac was obliged to grope in the dark.

Colin was thinking, too. He was determined not to say that he knew where the hummel was. It seemed to him that there would be much more honour and glory about the affair if they were to come upon their quarry by accident – and Colin wanted honour and glory! It was a poor sort of thing to go out and shoot a beast that was grazing peacefully in a meadow – a beast that was waiting for you to come. You might as well shoot a sheep, thought Colin contemptuously.

The third member of the little party had been watching his companions with interest and some amusement. He knew very little about the conditions of the forest but he knew quite a lot about human beings and Colin's face was

not difficult to read. Gerald felt pretty certain that Colin
had seen the hummel – or at least that Colin knew exactly
where the beast was.

'Listen, Mac!' said Gerald. 'What about trying Colin's
way first? If the hummel isn't there we can easily go up the
hill afterwards, can't we?'

'That is the thing to do,' said Colin eagerly. 'The beast will
be going after the hinds down by the river. Yes, indeed, that
is what he will be doing. We must go after him: Mister
Gerald is right.'

Mac was still dubious about it but he gave in so they
turned and worked their way across the shoulder of the
hill, climbing amongst rocks and scrambling down screes,
and presently found themselves in the throat of the gulley
leading from Tigh na Feidh to the river. The wind, which
had been blowing steadily on their left cheeks, now swirled
up behind them and whistled through the narrow cleft with
a strange moaning sound.

Gerald had been here before, of course (Mac had brought
him through the Black Pass in the Land-Rover) but today he
was on his two feet so he was able to look about him and
to see it better. As a matter of fact by dint of studying
Malcolm's map and marking the salient features he was
beginning to get the lie of the land.

'This is a grim sort of place,' he remarked.

'Yes, it's a bit eerie,' agreed Mac. 'It's worse at night, of
course. None of the villagers will come through the Black
Pass after dark, will they, Colin?'

'They would not like to come alone,' agreed Colin.
'They are saying it is haunted by a ghost that moans and
groans, but I am thinking it is just the wind whistling
amongst the rocks that is moaning and groaning.'

This was probably true, thought Gerald, but all the same
there was something horrible about the place. The high
black cliffs were dripping with moisture and green slimy

vegetation, the narrow road wound tortuously between boulders which had fallen from the heights.

Fortunately the Pass was little more than a hundred and fifty yards long, so they soon emerged from the gloom into bright sunshine. They left the boy and the pony and went down the hill towards the river. There was still no sign of the hummel. Mac, who had been annoyed before, began to feel angry. (If Colin had gulled them into coming all this way to no purpose – well – Colin should hear of it, thought Mac!)

But Colin was striding along as if he knew exactly where he was going and Gerald was following him so after a moment's hesitation Mac fell into line.

It was warmer now for they were sheltered from the wind by the barrier of rocks at their backs. Before them lay the river, winding along peacefully in the sunshine. On this side of the river lay an undulating meadow with small knolls crowned with bushes and scattered clumps of trees. It was here that the hinds loved to feed. (Mac wondered why there were no hinds feeding here this morning.) The river was the march of the MacAslan property, beyond it the ground belonged to Glen Veigh.

The sheltered valley surprised Gerald. It was so different from the rest of Ard na Feidh and such a complete contrast to the rocky gorge! Here one could easily imagine oneself in an English meadow: the lush grass, the trees and bushes, the winding river were all in keeping with the idea. The diversity of the scenery in Scotland is part of its charm. Where else could one find the rugged majesty of crag and torrent and the smiling peace of watered pastures within a morning's walk?

Colin led the way downstream for about half a mile and left his two gentlemen to have their lunch in the shelter of a group of trees while he went on to reconnoitre. It was just here that the boys had seen the hummel and it would never do to walk into him unprepared. The beast was probably resting in the lee of a knoll, chewing the cud and meditating upon the foolishness of his hunters.

Colin crawled along by the river's edge, taking cover beneath the overhanging bank; he was walking in the water most of the time – but what of that? The only thing that mattered was the hummel. So far Colin's plan had been successful (it had been a good plan).

Young MacAslan would be pleased with him and would keep him on at Ard na Feidh. Mother would be pleased, too, thought Colin, smiling to himself. Presently he raised his head very cautiously and peeped over the river-bank and . . . oh joy! . . . there was the hummel, grazing in the meadow. It was a huge creature – even bigger than Colin had thought – with massive shoulders and a thick ugly neck!

Colin grinned with delight. It was grand. He was so pleased that he almost forgot to look round and make up his mind where young MacAslan was to shoot from – almost, but not quite. The creature was a good bit farther down the meadow and not more than a hundred yards from the river-bank – a nice shot, thought Colin. He wetted his finger and held it up to test the wind. The wind had veered slightly but not enough to matter; it was still coming off the hill towards the river, so that was all right too.

There was a small bluff covered with brambles on the bank of the river and therefore about a hundred yards from the beast. That obviously was the place. Colin looked at the hummel again: the beast was grazing quietly. Everything was fine!

Colin went back to the two gentlemen as quickly as he could and made his announcement:

'The hornless beast is in the meadow. It is just as I was thinking,' said Colin with justifiable pride.

Mac could scarcely believe his ears. 'Are you sure?' he asked incredulously.

'I have seen him. He is grazing peacefully but it will be better to go at once.'

They rose, packed up the remains of their lunch, and Gerald took off his rain-coat.

'I'm coming to see the fun,' Gerald explained.

'You take him, Gerald,' said Mac generously.

'No, you! I want to see you kill him, that's all.'

They argued amicably as they followed Colin down to the river. It was finally decided that Mac should have the honour of despatching the hornless stag to the Forests of Paradise.

'We must be keeping well down under the bank,' Colin warned them. 'I have the place marked. It is a little knoll with brambles on the top. When we get there I will be holding up my hand.'

Mac nodded. Colin had taken charge and, if things were really as he said, he had taken charge to some purpose! Mac made sure that his rifle was ready and followed Colin into the river.

It was a wet passage. Sometimes the river curved into the bank and they were obliged to wade, waist-deep in the water; sometimes the stream curved towards the opposite bank, leaving exposed a narrow strand of gravel; sometimes the bank was so low that they had to bend down and crawl along on their hands and feet.

At last Colin stopped and held up his hand. The bank was high and fairly steep at this point and was covered with brambles. Mac climbed up very carefully and found himself on the bluff. The brambles scratched his hands and knees and tore his kilt but he was too excited to care. He edged himself along, lying on his face and pushing his rifle in front of him. As he neared the top he felt the wind lift his hair: his forehead was damp with perspiration and the wind felt very cold. It was blowing straight down off the hills so there was no chance of the hummel's scenting him.

Mac raised his head and peered through the screen of brambles – and was transfixed with amazement at what he saw: the hummel was coming straight towards him at a gallop!

For a moment Mac believed that the beast meant to attack him, it was charging him! But no, how could it be charging? Mac was hidden from sight in the brambles and the wind was blowing directly in his face. The beast couldn't possibly have known he was there. Something must have frightened the creature and he was running away like all his tribe. There must be somebody on the hill ...

All this passed through Mac's brain in a flash.

The question was: what should he do?

Would a bullet penetrate that hard bony head? Would it?

Mac's finger was on the trigger. He hesitated. By this time the beast was almost on him: he could see the great coarse hornless head; the strange lumps where the horns should have been; he could see the whites of the frightened eyes!

Quick! said his brain. You must do something quickly. It was too late now: the hummel was too near to shoot. Mac raised himself on to his knees, the beast saw him . . . and stopped dead. They gazed at each other, face to face, for a second. Then, with a snort of terror the hummel swerved and galloped madly down the meadow. A sod of earth, thrown up by its hoof, struck Mac on the forehead.

Mac was too dazed to shoot . . . and anyhow, even if he managed to hit the flying flank it would only have wounded the creature and Mac never shot a stag unless he could be sure of killing it; wounded stags sometimes run for miles before they can be followed up and despatched.

'Good lord!' exclaimed a voice at Mac's side. 'I thought the beast was going to attack you.'

'So did I,' Mac admitted. 'It gave me an awful fright. It seemed so uncanny, somehow. You don't expect a stag to attack you! For a moment I thought the brute couldn't be a stag at all! I didn't know whether to shoot or not,' he added apologetically.

'You were right not to shoot,' declared Gerald.

Colin was of a different opinion; he was bitterly disappointed at the hummel's escape. 'Och, you should have shot him!' cried Colin. 'You should have shot him when you had the chance.'

'But he hadn't the chance,' objected Gerald. 'The creature was coming straight at him and it would have taken a very heavy bullet to penetrate that bony skull.'

'I might have got his eye,' Mac pointed out. He was annoyed with himself: perhaps he should have risked a shot. It was not as if the beast was a good stag. They wanted the hummel killed.

'It would have been a fluke if you had got his eye,' Gerald declared. 'You couldn't possibly have been certain of getting a vital spot in an animal that was coming at you full gallop.'

'That's twice I've missed the chance of killing him,' said Mac in mournful tones.

'Third time lucky,' suggested Gerald consolingly.

'Maybe not,' put in Colin. 'I am thinking he will be away back over the river to Glen Veigh.'

This was not improbable. The creature had been so terrified that he was unlikely to stop running until he had put as many miles as possible between himself and his hunters. Anyhow there was nothing more that could be done today.

'He wasn't really charging you, was he?' asked Gerald, as they walked back across the meadow to the clump of trees where they had left their coats.

'No, he wasn't,' Mac replied. 'He couldn't have known I was there . . . and in any case I've never heard of a stag charging anybody. Something must have scared him. There must be somebody on the hill. Don't you think so, Colin?'

Colin agreed. He had been wondering if it could have been his brothers – but he could not believe the boys would be so foolish. They knew too much about the peculiarities of deer to allow the hummel to get wind of them. Yet, who else could it be? He unslung his glass and scanned the hillside for some movement which would betray the presence of a human being but there was nothing to be seen.

By this time they had reached the place where they had left their coats and, almost at once, a huge cloud appeared over the hills and a thin misty drizzle began to fall.

'This is an extraordinary climate!' Gerald exclaimed as he turned up the collar of his leather jacket. 'At three o'clock there wasn't a cloud in the sky – I should have said there was no chance of rain for days – and look at it now!'

'I'm used to the sudden changes,' Mac declared. He said it somewhat truculently and Gerald could not help smiling: he had noticed that Mac and Phil were both up in arms in a moment at the slightest aspersion upon their beloved Ard na Feidh.

'I wasn't complaining,' Gerald said mildly. 'As a matter of fact I find the sudden changes pleasant. In Africa I got bored to death with the weather. It continued for weeks on end without a change. I used to long for rain. Not heavy tropical rain, but a misty drizzle just like this.'

'You will be wanting your coat,' said Colin, picking it up off the ground.

'No, I don't want it,' Gerald replied. 'I'm wet already . . . and I've just told you I like the rain. Perhaps you'd like to put it on yourself, Colin. You look cold.'

Colin was cold. He had not got his plaid (he had left it with the boys) and his clothes were old and worn so there was not much warmth in them. 'Well,' he said doubtfully. 'Well . . . if you would not be wanting it yourself, Mister Gerald . . .'

'Put it on; it will save you carrying it,' said Gerald, smiling.

Colin put it on. He was too hot now but he was so pleased with his appearance that he could not bear to take it off. He put on the cap as well. Perhaps some day he would be able to afford to buy a coat and cap like this, thought Colin, smiling to himself as he followed the two gentlemen up the hill. Today had been very disappointing but he was not really worrying; he thought young MacAslan was too fair-minded to blame him for what was not his fault. It appeared that he was right.

When they reached the Black Pass the two gentlemen stopped.

'Come here, Colin,' said Mac. 'I want to speak to you. I don't know how you guessed that the hummel was there, but—'

'It was just an idea I was having.'

'Well, it was a good idea,' admitted Mac. 'I'd have got him if he hadn't been scared by somebody on the hill. I'm very pleased with you, Colin. I shall tell MacAslan exactly what happened and he'll be pleased too.'

'I was thinking,' said Colin, a little diffidently. 'I was thinking that if the hornless stag was away back to Glen Veigh I would be seeing his slots on the edge of the river. He is a heavy beast and his slots would be big and easy to see. I was thinking that if he was not going back to Glen Veigh we might be having another try at him.'

Mac saw the point. 'Yes, that's a good plan, Colin. If this mist clears tomorrow you can walk along the edge of the river and see if you can find the place where he crossed over. If he hasn't crossed the river he must be here.'

'That is what I was thinking,' agreed Colin eagerly. 'If he is here we will be finding him on the hill.'

They walked on together making plans. Gerald followed with the boy and the pony. Gerald was interested in the Shetland ponies and wanted to know more about them, but the boy was shy and appeared to have difficulty in understanding what Gerald said to him and even more difficulty in replying to the simplest question. It seemed strange to Gerald that a boy who had lived all his life in the British Isles could scarcely speak a word of English.

The mist, which at first had been gauzy and insubstantial, was now thickening and heavy clouds were massing behind the hills so by the time they had reached the Black Pass it was difficult to see where they were going. The wind had fallen to a gentle breeze so that the mist swirled and eddied: at one moment you could see the cliffs towering grim and black at either side and the next moment they were blotted out.

Gerald had just decided to hurry on and overtake Mac and Colin when he heard the sound of heavy boots on the stony ground and saw two shadowy figures leap from behind the boulders. One of them had some sort of weapon in his hand and struck Colin on the head. Colin threw up his arms and went down like a log.

There was a scrimmage . . . somebody shouted . . . Gerald ran forward but before he got to the scene of the attack the two shadowy figures had made off and disappeared in the mist. He found Mac kneeling beside Colin trying to lift his head from the ground.

'What on earth happened?' asked Gerald.

'They've killed him!' cried Mac. 'Gerald, they've killed him!'

'Who was it?'

'I don't know. I couldn't see them properly in this hellish mist. Ought we to go after them?'

'No, we must keep together. Let's see if Colin is badly injured.'

'He's dead!'

'No, no! His heart is beating quite strongly.'

'Thank God!' said Mac in trembling tones. 'I tried to feel his heart – but I couldn't. I thought he was dead. Who could it have been? Who could have done it – and why? I knew nothing until I heard the rattle of stones and the two figures loomed out of the mist. One of them hit Colin on the head. The next moment Colin stumbled and fell. I tried to get hold of the chap but he tore himself out of my grasp and ran away.'

'They shouted,' said Gerald.

'It was the other man who shouted, "You fool, he's got red hair!" Then they just . . . sort of vanished in the mist. Oh Gerald, what are we to do? We can't leave Colin here and go for help.'

'Call for the boy to bring the pony. You can do that, can't you? He doesn't seem to understand a word of English. We must take Colin up to the house. He's wet and cold so the sooner we get him to bed the better. We can't take him home tonight.'

Mac shouted to the boy. His voice was hoarse and echoed amongst the overhanging cliffs (the narrow defile was full of echoes). After a few minutes the boy appeared, leading the pony. The boy was as white as a sheet; he looked terrified!

Meanwhile Gerald had examined Colin. There had been accidents at Koolbokie and Gerald had often helped the doctor so he knew a good deal about First Aid and he was relieved to discover that Colin's injury was not serious. The blow had fallen on the back of his head but his hair was extremely thick and he had been wearing a cap so the skin was not broken. He had been stunned, that was all; already he had begun to recover his senses. He moaned and opened his eyes and clutched Gerald's arm.

'It's all right, Colin,' said Gerald comfortingly. 'You got a bash on the head. Just lie still for a minute or two. You'll soon feel better.'

'It was Euan,' muttered Colin, trying to struggle to his feet. 'It was Euan, the dirty skunk!' Then his muttering changed from English to Gaelic and he uttered a string of what sounded like fearsome threats and imprecations.

'Wait,' said Gerald, holding him down. 'Stay where you are and rest for a few minutes.'

'Where is Euan? Let me get at him!' Then came another burst of Gaelic which sounded even more fearsome than before.

'There doesn't seem to be much wrong with him,' said Mac with a sigh of relief.

'He may have concussion,' Gerald replied.

They lifted Colin on to the pony and set out for Tigh na Feidh; Mac walked on one side and Gerald on the other. The pony was so small that they were able to support Colin with their arms round his shoulders. Most of the time he was limp and quiet but every now and then he struggled and tried to get off and raved in Gaelic.

Mac was thankful when they left the Black Pass behind them; his brain was busy in a dazed sort of way: what ought he to do? He must tell the police as soon as possible – and he must tell Colin's mother. She would hear about the accident of course. News of this kind got about quickly in Ardfalloch . . . and, like a snowball rolling downhill, it always gathered weight.

'Look here, Gerald,' said Mac. 'I shall have to send somebody down to the village tonight. We must let Mrs MacTaggart know what has happened and we must ring up the police. We ought to have gone after that fellow and found out who he was. Then we could have told the police—'

'We couldn't,' interrupted Gerald. 'We couldn't possibly have found anybody amongst the rocks in that mist. It would have been madness to try. We should have had to leave Colin alone and the thug might have returned and finished him off. The only sensible thing to do was to stay together. I agree that Colin's mother ought to be told but who can you send?'

'I could send the two pony boys,' replied Mac doubtfully.

'Wouldn't they get lost in the mist?'

'Not if they keep to the path. They're both local boys so they know their way about . . . but they couldn't ring up the police.'

'I'll go if you like.'

'No,' said Mac firmly. 'You'd just get lost. Besides you seem to know about First Aid. I don't know anything about it. Perhaps we should send for Doctor Wedderburn. Oh gosh, I wish I knew what to do!' added Mac, in despair.

19   In which Mac boils over

By this time Gerald and Mac – with Colin on the pony – had arrived at Tigh na Feidh. Old Kirsty was there and received them with lamentations: 'Och, what has happened? Och, the puir laddie! Has he been shot? He's as white as a ghost! Is he dying?'

'No, he isn't dying,' replied Gerald. 'There has been a slight accident, that's all. Fill some hot-water-bottles; boil a kettle and make tea. Be as quick as you can.'

Gerald spoke with so much authority that the old woman was silenced and hurried off to the kitchen. Meanwhile Gerald and Mac attended to Colin. They carried him upstairs, took off his clothes, rubbed him with warm towels and put him into bed between blankets.

'You know what to do,' said Mac with a sigh of relief.

'It's just common sense,' replied Gerald. 'He's cold and wet. We don't want him to get pneumonia.'

All this time there had been no sign of the girls, so when Kirsty came with the tea and the hot-water-bottles Mac asked her where they were.

Kirsty replied with more lamentations: they had gone out after lunch (she had told them not to go, but they would not heed her). They had got lost in the mist! They had fallen over a precipice and broken their legs; Malcolm and Mr Stoddart had not come back either; she was sure something dreadful had happened.

'Och, it is a black day!' wailed Kirsty, wringing her hands. 'It is a black day, so it is! I was dreaming of a black horse last night. A huge black horse came out of the river all dreeping wet with wotter. I was telling Malcolm but he would not be listening to me. It is a sure sign of trouble to be dreaming of a black horse . . .'

Mac was not worried about Malcolm and Oliver (Malcolm knew every yard of the forest and was unlikely to get lost) but he was extremely worried about Phil and Donny. He was worried about Colin, too.

'Gerald, he looks dreadfully ill,' said Mac in alarm. 'Shouldn't we get the doctor?'

'How can we?' asked Gerald. 'It would be difficult for him to get here . . . and he would only tell us to keep the patient warm and give him hot drinks. But you had better let Colin's mother know not to expect him home.'

'What about the police?'

'I should wait, if I were you. We don't want a lot of fuss until we can make up our minds what really happened. Play it down, that's my advice. It will be time enough to ring up the police tomorrow morning.'

'It was Euan,' raved Colin. 'I am not wanting the police. I will be after Euan myself with a big stick . . .'

Mac went downstairs and wrote a short letter to Mrs MacTaggart. He told her that Colin was staying at Tigh na Feidh for the night – that was all. It was no good frightening the woman unnecessarily.

Mac, himself, was upset and frightened. The whole day had been 'queer': first there had been Colin's insistence that they would find the hummel in the meadow beyond the Black Pass (a most unlikely place); then the surprise of finding him there; then the hummel's extraordinary behaviour . . . and then, to cap all, the attack in the Black Pass!

Mac realised now that the men who had attacked Colin were probably the cause of the hummel's fright. Yes, thought Mac. That clears up *that* mystery. They must have been on the hill, watching for Colin, and the beast got a whiff of their scent. Then they must have worked their way along and waited for us in the Pass.

It was getting late now and still there was no sign of the wanderers! By this time Mac was nearly off his head with anxiety. He kept on opening the front door and peering into the mist . . . and listening. If he had had the slightest idea which way the girls had gone he would have put on his coat and sallied forth to look for them, but he hadn't, of course, so there was nothing to be done. He had just made up his mind to go and consult Gerald when he heard footsteps on the gravel-drive and the whole party loomed out of the misty darkness.

Mac shouted and Malcolm replied. The next moment they walked in at the door: Malcolm and Phil and Donny and a somewhat bedraggled Oliver bringing up the rear.

'Good heavens! What happened?' exclaimed Mac. Now that they were all here – and safe – his anxiety changed to wrath.

'Nothing much,' replied Phil. 'You weren't worrying, were you?'

'Not in the least. Why should I worry? I just thought you were lost, that's all. Kirsty dreamt about a black horse "all dreeping wet with wotter" so she was certain you had fallen over a precipice and broken your legs. I suppose you know it's after eight o'clock?'

'I'm sorry, Mac,' said Phil remorsefully. 'I'm awfully sorry. My watch stopped so I didn't realise it was so late. It was a lovely afternoon so Donny and I went out for our usual walk and the mist came down so suddenly that we were taken by surprise. We wandered about for a bit and then we met the boy with the pony so we waited for Oliver and Malcolm and all came home together.' She added, 'We're a bit wet so we'll go and change. If you're hungry you can start supper without us.'

Mac was not hungry so he did not reply.

They ran upstairs to change . . . all except Malcolm who lingered in the hall with a very glum expression upon his face. Mac turned to him and said, 'What's wrong with you?'

'I am wanting to speak to you, Mac,' the man replied. 'There was a little disagreement between Mister Stoddart and me. He will be telling you his story and maybe it will be a wee bit different from my story. It was this way—'

'I'll hear your story later,' interrupted Mac. 'Meanwhile somebody must go down to the village with this letter. It's to tell Mrs MacTaggart that Colin is staying here for the night.'

'Colin is staying here?' asked Malcolm in amazement.

'Yes, he's not well.'

'Och, what did I tell you? He is no good, that one! He would trip over his own feet!'

'He didn't "trip over his own feet". He did very well indeed. I was pleased with him – and told him so.'

'Were you seeing the hummel at all?'

'Yes, and it wasn't Colin's fault that we didn't get him. There's no time to tell you about it now; I want this letter to go to Mrs MacTaggart at once.'

'Who is to take it?'

'You can send the two pony-boys,' replied Mac. 'They can take Queenie; she'll find her way home all right.'

'Och, there is no need for all that fuss,' grumbled Malcolm. 'I have had a long weary day and I am wanting my supper . . . and the boys will be rubbing down the ponies. They will not be best pleased if I am telling them that they must be going down to the village tonight. It will do well enough if they are taking the letter in the morning.'

Mac boiled over. 'Do as you're told and hurry up about it,' he shouted. Then he turned, walked into the dining-room, and shut the door.

It was what his father would have done (if Malcolm had dared to object to an order from MacAslan) but all the same, Mac was a little worried so he peeped out of the window from behind the curtain and was relieved to see Malcolm's thickset figure hastening round the corner of the house towards the stables.

20 Is concerned with a serious inquiry

Mac threw himself into a big chair near the fire and flung his legs over the arm. It was a favourite position of his when he was feeling tired. He was very tired indeed so he was not pleased when Oliver appeared and began his tale of woe.

'Listen, Mac,' said Oliver earnestly. 'I want to speak to you before the others come down. That man is insufferable. He thinks he's indispensable and can do as he likes.'

'Do you mean Malcolm?'

'Yes, of course! It's HIS forest and HIS deer. He thinks the whole place belongs to him. You ought to sack him.'

'I ought to sack Malcolm? My dear chap, Malcolm was here before I was born!'

'That's just what I mean,' urged Oliver. 'He has been here far too long. Lucius Cottar always says that when a man begins to think he's indispensable . . .'

'Well, I can't sack him,' interrupted Mac. 'The only person who can sack Malcolm is MacAslan – and he wouldn't dream of doing any such thing. See?'

'Listen, Mac,' repeated Oliver. 'I want to tell you exactly what happened. We spotted the Royal quite early in the day and stalked him for hours. Then we lost him. I was fed up, I can tell you. He was a fine young beast with a beautiful head – just what I want! Lucius Cottar has a Royal but his Royal is no finer.'

'How nice!'

'It was four o'clock by that time,' continued Oliver. 'I wanted to have another look round but there was a slight gauzy sort of cloud over Ben Ghaoth and Malcolm declared that it would spread and thicken so I gave in and we started home. Then, quite by accident, we came across the stag. He was in a little valley near a burn, grazing peacefully. It was a narrow valley with rocks on either side: that was why we hadn't seen him before. He was well within range – an easy shot! – but, can you believe it? Malcolm refused to let me kill him.'

'Malcolm refused—'

'Yes, refused, point-blank! He said the visibility was too poor (there were only a few shreds of gauzy mist drifting up the valley)! He said it was difficult to shoot a stag from above! He said he "was not wanting to spend all night on the hill searching for a wounded stag". What do you think of that?'

'You must have riled him,' said Mac, hiding a smile.

'Riled him!' exclaimed Oliver. 'I was properly riled! I've never been so insulted in my life. I told him I wasn't in the habit of wounding stags but he just turned his back and walked off. If I had had my rifle I could have killed the stag quite easily.'

'If you had had your rifle?' asked Mac.

'Malcolm was carrying it for me,' Oliver explained.

Mac visualised the scene and began to shake with internal laughter. He was doing his best to stifle it when Kirsty came in with the supper, followed by Gerald and the girls. The situation was saved!

At supper the talk turned to the experiences of Mac and Gerald, the behaviour of the hummel and the attack in the Pass. Mac had decided to walk down to the village the following morning and put the whole matter into the hands of the police. He knew Major Kane and liked him so he would speak to him personally.

'What nonsense!' exclaimed Oliver. 'Major Kane would

laugh at you! It was the result of a fight in the village. You don't go running to the police every time there's a fight and one of the chaps gets a black eye.'

'But it wasn't a "black eye",' Mac pointed out. 'It wasn't a fight either. It was a deliberate attack on an unsuspecting man. In fact it was an ambush.'

'An "ambush"!' said Oliver scornfully.

'Well, what else can you call it?' asked Phil. 'Mac says the two men were lying in wait for Colin. That's an ambush, isn't it?'

'Mac doesn't know—' began Oliver.

'What do you mean?' interrupted Mac. 'I was there and saw it happen.'

'You couldn't see much in that fog. You said so yourself, didn't you?'

'But Gerald saw them too! Didn't you Gerald?'

'Yes,' said Gerald. 'They were disappearing when I saw them. They were just two shadowy figures but I heard their feet clattering on the stones.'

'You'll have to have a better story than that if you want the police to take action,' Oliver declared.

'A better story!' cried Mac. 'How can we have "a better story"? All we can tell the police is the true story of what happened.'

'It's so vague,' complained Oliver.

'It happened in a fog,' Gerald pointed out.

The atmosphere was becoming extremely heated. Donny, who was always for peace, tried to change the subject by asking what Colin was to have for supper.

'Nothing solid,' said Gerald. 'He could have milk pudding, or something like that.'

'There's a tin of milk pudding in the store-cupboard,' said Phil. 'I'll prepare it and give it to him. He had better have it now—'

'I'll do it!' suggested Donny.

'No, don't worry! I know where it is. It won't take long.' Phil rose and went away to find it.

By this time the meal was finished so the others moved over to the chairs near the fire; Kirsty came in to clear the table and as usual proceeded to collect the various garments and other impedimenta which were strewn about the room. When she had said 'good night' and had gone away Oliver remarked, 'This room is always disgracefully untidy. I don't know how that woman can bear it.'

'Oh, Kirsty doesn't mind; she's used to our ways,' replied Mac.

'I like it,' declared Donny. 'It's so restful if you don't have to be tidy and punctual.'

Gerald agreed with her (he, too, enjoyed the easy-going ways which obtained at Tigh na Feidh) but it was obvious from Oliver's expression that he disagreed profoundly.

'What about your friend, Lucius Cottar?' inquired Mac.

'His house is always in perfect order,' replied Oliver, rising to the bait. 'I think I told you that he has a house near Ascot with a couple to look after it. They have been with him for years. Crumbleworth is a well-trained butler and valet; Mrs Crumbleworth is a marvellous cook and they are both so trustworthy that Lucius can leave them in charge of the place and go away for months with an easy mind . . .'

'Like Bunter,' murmured Donny, dreamily.

'But Bunter wasn't married,' whispered Gerald.

'He combined the perfections of Mr and Mrs Crumbleworth in his own person,' returned Donny in the same muted tones.

Oliver was still holding forth about the perfections of the Crumbleworths (and Mac had begun to regret his mischievous question) when Phil returned. She reported that Colin seemed much better, he had eaten his pudding and had settled down for the night.

'He still thinks it was Euan Dalgliesh who attacked him,' added Phil. 'But it couldn't have been, of course.'

'Why not?' asked Mac. 'Colin is sure it was Euan. They had a fight the other day and Euan got the worst of it, so—'

'There, I told you!' interrupted Oliver. 'I told you it was the result of a fight in the village, didn't I? What fools you would have looked if you had gone to the police!'

'It wasn't Euan,' said Phil.

'But Colin says—'

'It wasn't Euan,' repeated Phil firmly. 'Euan Dalgliesh is a nice lad. Oh, I dare say they had a fight: they're both red-headed and they're both rather keen on that girl who helps Mrs MacTaggart in the kitchen. I can imagine them going for each other, hammer and tongs, but I can't imagine Euan hiding behind a rock and hitting Colin on the back of his head.'

'No,' said Mac, thoughtfully. 'No, you're right, Phil.'

'Besides, there were two of them,' Phil pointed out. 'That makes it even nastier, doesn't it?'

'Let us talk it over thoroughly,' suggested Oliver, leaning back in his chair and placing his fingers tip to tip. 'We're all here – all five of us. Let us examine the possibilities in cold blood. That's the best way to get to the bottom of the affair. It isn't any good getting angry – like Mac – that doesn't help. We must all keep perfectly cool and calm. Phil says it wasn't Euan—'

'It wasn't Euan,' interrupted Phil.

' "What I tell you three times is true",' quoted Mac under his breath.

Oliver took no notice of the interruption. He said, 'Well, if it wasn't Euan, who was it? That's what we've got to decide. We want constructive ideas so that we can discuss them frankly and come to some conclusion. Phil says it wasn't Euan – but she hasn't put forward any other solution to the problem,' added Oliver, smiling superciliously.

'It might have been you,' Phil suggested.

Oliver's smile vanished. He said coldly, 'I have an alibi. I was with Malcolm all day.'

'You and Malcolm were in cahoots. That's the solution, of course! Malcolm wants Colin's job for his cousin; he explains the matter to you and you agree to help him. You hide behind a boulder and hit Colin on the head while Malcolm stands guard . . . or perhaps Malcolm hits him on the head and you stand guard. What about that, Oliver? Or of course the ambush might have been planned and carried out by Donny and me: we were wandering about in the mist for hours! We lurk in the Pass, I pick up a large stone and bash Colin on the head. Then we both run for our lives. I don't quite know why I wanted to bash Colin. Perhaps it was just a sudden fit of homicidal mania, or perhaps—'

'When you have quite finished talking nonsense we'll get on with our inquiry,' interrupted Oliver. He pursed his lips and waited.

There was a short silence.

'Go on,' said Mac. 'Go on, Oliver. What's your theory?'

'It could have been Burleigh Brown. He's the most likely person.'

'Me?' asked Gerald in astonishment.

'You had the best opportunity,' Oliver pointed out. 'You were walking behind Colin. You could have run forward and laid him out and dodged behind a rock, then you could have come out and asked Mac what had happened.'

'But look here—' began Gerald.

'Oh, I'm not saying it *was* you. I'm just saying it might have been you,' Oliver explained. 'We agreed to examine all the possibilities in cold blood, didn't we? By the way, Phil mentioned "a large stone". That's the first I've heard of any weapon being used in the attack.'

'It was a blunt instrument,' said Mac. 'It's always a blunt instrument.'

'Do you mean you saw the weapon or are you just trying to be funny?'

'I'm just trying to think,' replied Mac quite seriously. 'I've got a sort of impression that the chap had something in his hand.'

'It was a spanner,' said Gerald.

'You mean you saw it?'

'Yes, that's exactly what I mean.'

'That's important,' Oliver declared. 'We ought to find it. The spanner will have the man's fingerprints on it. The police can identify a man by his fingerprints.'

'We all know that,' said Mac. 'I don't suppose there's a schoolchild over the age of ten who doesn't know that a man can be identified by his fingerprints.'

'You may be interested to know that the spanner in question will have my fingerprints on it,' said Gerald cheerfully.

'Your fingerprints?' asked Oliver.

'Yes. I found it lying on the ground when I was examining Colin so I picked it up and brought it home with me and put it over there – on that chair.'

'We ought to lock it up safely and keep it for the police,' Oliver declared. He rose, looked at the chair, and added, 'It isn't there now. Are you sure you put it there?'

'Perfectly certain.'

'Oh, *that* was the spanner!' Phil exclaimed. 'Kirsty showed me a dirty old spanner when I was in the kitchen preparing Colin's pudding. She said she had found it when she was tidying up the room. I told her to give it to Malcolm: I didn't know that there was anything important about it.'

'We must get it from Malcolm and lock it up.'

Mac began to chuckle. 'Malcolm will have cleaned it thoroughly by this time – if I know anything about him.

There's nothing Malcolm likes better than cleaning things. You can go and ask him if you like.'

Oliver rose reluctantly (he was not very good friends with Malcolm at the moment). He paused at the door and announced, 'If this were Lucius Cottar's house he would ring for the man.'

'Of course,' agreed Mac. 'He has electric bells in every room. He has only to press the button and Crumbleforth appears, like the genie in the story of Aladdin. I've often thought I should like to possess a wonderful lamp.'

Oliver made no reply to this childish nonsense. He went out and shut the door behind him.

This seemed to Gerald a good opportunity of clearing up a point which had been exercising his mind. 'Have any of you ever seen Lucius Cottar?' he inquired.

'None of us has ever seen him,' replied Mac.

'But he's quite real – if that's what you mean,' declared Phil. 'I can "see" Lucius Cottar if I shut my eyes: he's tall and thin, with sleek black hair receding from his forehead—'

'Sticking out teeth and no chin,' put in Mac vindictively.

'His feet are so long and narrow that he has to have his shoes specially made for him,' said Donny. She added, 'That's true, you know. Oliver told me.'

'He has his hands manicured once a fortnight,' announced Phil.

'Except when he's shooting lions,' Mac reminded her.

They had all been perfectly serious but now, with one accord, they burst into gales of laughter. Gerald laughed too, but all the same, Lucius Cottar had become 'real' to him.

They were still laughing uproariously when Oliver returned. 'Malcolm showed me the spanner,' said Oliver. 'He had cleaned it and oiled it and put it away. I don't know why you're laughing. It's no laughing matter.'

'It is to me,' gasped Mac. 'But I have a very keen sense – of humour.'

'Your sense of humour is rather too keen,' his sister told him.

'Oh, I know,' agreed Mac. 'My sense of humour gets me into awful trouble sometimes . . . but I can't help it. It's the way I'm made.'

'Kirsty had no right to remove the spanner,' declared Oliver. 'She ought to have asked—'

'But, Oliver!' interrupted Mac. 'You're always saying that this room is "disgracefully untidy" and now you're annoyed with poor old Kirsty for tidying up.'

'Do you want to get on with this inquiry or not?' asked Oliver raising his voice.

'Let's hear what he has to say,' suggested Gerald. 'I'd like to know why he picked on me as the villain of the piece.'

Oliver resumed his position in the chair nearest to the fire. 'Very well,' he said. 'I don't mind conducting the inquiry but you must be sensible about it. I suggested Burleigh Brown for several reasons. He had the best opportunity; he handled the spanner and admits that his fingerprints were on it (he didn't know Malcolm had cleaned it so he had to make up some excuse); last but not least he had a very good motive.'

'What was my motive?' asked Gerald in surprise.

'You wanted to silence him.'

'Silence him?'

'Yes. Perhaps he knows too much about you.'

'What on earth do you mean?' asked Mac.

'Ask him,' replied Oliver, pointing at Gerald. 'Ask him why he left Koolbokie Mine in a hurry. If he won't tell you, I will. He was sacked for stealing diamonds.'

'What nonsense!' exclaimed Phil angrily. 'I don't know where you can have heard such a ridiculous story—'

'It's true, Phil.'

'I don't believe a word of it!'

'Oh, it's quite true,'said Gerald. 'I was sacked for stealing diamonds. The diamonds were discovered hidden in the lining of my jacket so, naturally enough, I was dismissed then and there. Stoddart's information is perfectly correct as far as it goes. It's a little out-of-date, that's all. He doesn't seem to have heard the end of the story: Sir Walter Mac-Callum believed I was innocent so he sent his private detective to investigate the affair. The detective found out the truth; the thief was caught red-handed and was tried and sent to prison.'

Gerald's companions had been listening with bated breath – and with very different feelings.

'There! What did I tell you?' exclaimed Phil. 'I knew it wasn't true—'

'You've only got his word for it,' Oliver pointed out.

'Are you calling me a liar, Stoddart?' demanded Gerald, half-rising from his chair.

'No, of course not,' said Oliver hastily. 'I just meant – I mean I heard about it from – from someone. I suppose you've got proofs? I mean—'

'I don't want "proofs",' Phil interrupted.

'Nor I,' declared Mac.

'I have no proofs here,' Gerald told them. 'It never occurred to me to bring the letter, which I received from the manager of Koolbokie, when I was packing my suitcase to come to Ard na Feidh.'

'Of course not!' cried Phil. 'Why should you? Oliver is just being silly.'

Gerald took no notice of the interruption. He turned to Oliver and added, 'You can ring up Sir Walter MacCallum if you like.'

'There's no telephone,' said Oliver sulkily.

'No telephone!' exclaimed Mac. 'If there were fifty tele-phones I wouldn't ring up Sir Walter! Gerald's word is good enough for me. The whole thing is fantastic . . . and anyhow it has nothing whatever to do with the "inquiry" we're supposed to be holding.'

'How do you make that out?' inquired Oliver.

'Because it's senseless. To begin with how could Colin know anything about Gerald's private affairs? To go on with: if Gerald had wanted to "silence" Colin he certainly wouldn't have given the man a tap on the back of his head and then done all in his power to revive him. Furthermore I was there and saw what happened this afternoon. I've told you again and again that there were two men lurking behind boulders, one on each side of the track and that they sprang out and felled Colin and ran away. Gerald was behind us, walking with the pony-boy. You had better ask the pony-boy if you don't believe me.'

There was a short silence.

Gerald had recovered his temper by this time (it was pleasant to be so hotly defended by Phil and Mac). He said, 'Well, let's leave that for the moment. Let's have another opinion on the subject. You've all said your say except Donny. Donny has been sitting there, listening, and saying nothing. What does Donny think about it?'

'Me?' exclaimed Donny, blushing to find herself in the limelight. 'I don't know, really. I was just – just thinking. I often read detective stories – and one of the most important things in a detective story is that you ought to take all the facts into consideration when you're trying to find the solution to a crime. You shouldn't just take some of the facts and leave out others because they don't fit your theory. That's what Poirot says . . . and Alleyn . . . and Miss Silver. They all say it.'

'You mean we've left something out?' asked Mac.

'Yes,' said Donny, nodding. 'Yes, the man shouted. You said so, didn't you, Mac? You said the man shouted, "You fool, he's got red hair!" So it couldn't have been

Gerald, could it? It couldn't have been Euan Dalgliesh – or any of the local people – because they all know that Colin has red hair. It's the first thing you notice about Colin: he has the reddest hair I've ever seen in all my—'

'That isn't important,' interrupted Oliver. 'Besides it happened so suddenly and unexpectedly that Mac was taken by surprise. Mac might easily have been mistaken.'

'No,' said Mac, thoughtfully. 'No, I'm certain that was what he shouted. He shouted it in a surprised sort of way—'

'It couldn't have been that,' interrupted Oliver. 'It must have been something in Gaelic.'

'No, it wasn't. I know it seems unlikely but that was what he shouted: "You fool, he's got red hair!"'

'Was it the man who attacked Colin or the other man?' asked Gerald.

'The other man,' replied Mac without hesitation.

'That isn't important,' repeated Oliver. 'None of that has any bearing upon the case.'

'In a detective story everything is important,' said Donny. 'Every small detail has a bearing on the case.'

Mac had been thinking it over. He said, 'Donny is right, you know. It's very important indeed: it rules out everybody who knows Colin. The men who attacked Colin must have been strangers. Perhaps they were just a couple of tramps who wanted to pinch some money off us. MacTaggart said there were some queer types hanging about and making trouble in the village.'

'It couldn't have been that either,' said Phil.

'Why not?'

'Because, if they just wanted money, it wouldn't have mattered to them whether Colin's hair was red or black or yellow.' She rose and added, 'It has been a very long day. I'm dead tired and I'm going to bed. Are you coming, Donny?'

They went away together and Gerald followed them: he was anxious to escape before his companions noticed that he had not put forward any solution to the problem. He had thought – and thought – but he could find none that satisfied him. It was a mystery. It simply did not make sense.

Gerald looked in to see if Colin had all he wanted and found him sleeping peacefully. Then he, too, went to bed.

21 In which Mac is offered advice

Mac and Oliver were left alone, sitting by the fire. No sooner had the door shut behind the others than Oliver leaned forward and burst out: 'Mac, listen to me! There's something wrong about that fellow!'

'Something wrong? Do you mean he's not well?'

'No, I don't mean that at all. I mean there's something fishy about him. He isn't straight.'

'What rot! He's the straightest chap I've ever met. I like him immensely and so does Phil. I can't think why you've taken such a dislike to Gerald.'

'What do you know about him? You know nothing except what he has told you. Personally I don't believe a word of that story he told us tonight: about Sir Walter MacCallum sending the detective to Koolbokie.'

'You're talking nonsense, Oliver!'

'There you are! You just get angry when I try to talk to you.'

'I'm not angry,' declared Mac – not very truthfully. 'I'd just like to know this: what on earth would be the use of telling us a story which could be so easily disproved? You have only to ring up Sir Walter—'

'We can't. There's no telephone. We can't go down to the post office in this fog. Meanwhile—'

'Meanwhile I suppose Gerald walks off with the silver teaspoons in his pocket,' suggested Mac.

'You won't listen,' declared Oliver.

'I'm listening,' said Mac, throwing his legs over the arm of his chair. 'I'm listening, Oliver. Go ahead.'

Oliver accepted the invitation. 'Burleigh Brown is very plausible, I admit. You and Phil have been taken in by the man . . . but I'm older than you are and more experienced so you would do well to listen to what I have to say.'

'I'm listening.'

'It isn't the teaspoons he's after, it's Phil.'

'Phil? What do you mean?'

'Burleigh Brown is after Phil. I've been watching them: he's making up to her for all he's worth and she's infatuated with him. Oh, it's only a girlish infatuation – Phil is really quite sensible – but you ought to do something about it.'

Mac hesitated for a moment and then said, 'What do you propose I should do?'

'Well, to begin with you could listen to my advice without getting in a rage. I'm only telling you for your own good.'

There are few things more annoying than being told something 'for your own good'. 'Oh, how I wish Dad were here!' exclaimed Mac.

'If your father were here he would send that man packing in double quick time. That's what he would do.' Oliver leaned forward and continued, 'I'll tell you this – in confidence, of course – I asked Phil to marry me and she refused. I never was so surprised in my life.'

Mac was surprised too . . . but not for the same reason. He said, 'Good Lord, I had no idea you were – er – particularly keen on Phil! I thought you were a confirmed bachelor.'

'I was,' admitted Oliver. 'But just lately I decided to get married. Phil is pretty and attractive and (as I said before) she's really quite sensible so you can imagine how surprised I was when she refused to consider my offer. It's this silly girlish infatuation, of course. If you send that man away she'll soon get over it and come to her senses. I'm quite willing to wait,' added Oliver smugly.

Mac had been annoyed – he was still annoyed – but now, quite suddenly, his sense of humour got the upper hand and he was overcome by a fit of laughter. He tried to stifle it but it was uncontrollable. He roared with laughter . . .

'I see nothing funny about it,' declared Oliver. He rose in a dignified manner and left the room.

It was nearly midnight by this time and Mac was used to going to bed at ten. He was exhausted not only by the events of a long and tiring day but also by the various emotions which he had experienced. He had just risen and had put the guard on the fire when there was a tap on the door and Malcolm appeared.

'What on earth is the matter now?' groaned Mac.

'It is just that I was wanting to tell you my story,' Malcolm explained. 'You were saying you would hear my story later. So I was waiting.'

Mac remembered that he had used those very words; he sighed and sat down on the arm of a chair. 'All right, go on,' he said.

'I could tell you better in the Gaelic, Mac.'

'This was a "pose" of course: Malcolm could have told his story perfectly well in English. It was just that he thought MacAslan's son ought to have 'the Gaelic'. (Mac-Aslan's son thought otherwise.)

'But I couldn't be understanding better,' replied Mac with a little smile. 'Listen, Malcolm! I'll tell you what happened and you can stop me if I go wrong: you and Mr Stoddart stalked the Royal for hours; then he vanished. You had decided to come home when you discovered him grazing peacefully in a little valley with rocks all round. Mr Stoddart wanted to shoot the beast but you refused to let him. Then you turned—'

'It was a very deep corrie and it was full of mist,' interrupted Malcolm. 'There were wee puffs of air. At one moment you could be seeing the beast clearly and the next moment you could not be seeing him at all. We were above him on the side of the hill so it would have been a difficult shot even in clear weather. You are knowing, yourself, that it is not easy to kill a stag from above. It is MacAslan's rule that you should not be shooting unless you are sure of killing your stag – it is your rule too. It is a good rule.'

Mac nodded. 'But Mr Stoddart said it was an easy shot.'

'Mister Stoddart is quite a good shot but he is not as good as he thinks he is.'

'He said you were rude to him, Malcolm.'

'Maybe I was,' admitted Malcolm. 'I was a wee bit annoyed with Mister Stoddart. He is a very annoying gentleman.'

Mac felt like saying he couldn't agree more (he had been 'annoyed with Mister Stoddart' himself) but discipline had to be maintained so after a moment's thought he said, 'Well, it's a pity, but it can't be helped. I suppose you want me to write and tell MacAslan what happened?'

'That is what I am wanting,' replied Malcolm, smiling in relief.

As Mac went up the stairs to bed he decided that if anybody else wanted to talk to him tonight he would open his mouth and scream . . . but fortunately nobody did.

22 Is concerned with the arrival of a letter

The mist, which had come down so suddenly, persisted for two days. Sometimes it lifted for a few hours, sometimes it thickened, but the visibility was too poor for stalking.

Colin was better. He had a lump on the back of his head but he insisted on getting up and going home. Mac went with him to restore him to his mother and to tell her exactly what had happened. Mrs MacTaggart had heard a garbled account of the accident so she was delighted to see her son looking little the worse of his experience.

It was established that Colin's assailant could not have been Euan Dalgliesh as there had been a meeting of the Fire Brigade on Monday evening and Euan had been there. At least six lads of the village had seen him and spoken to him.

After his interview with Mrs MacTaggart Mac went to the inn and consulted Mr MacTaggart as to what he should do . . . and, as usual, Mr MacTaggart was delighted to offer advice.

'Och, I would wait for a bit,' said 'The Big Fish'. 'It would be a pity to bother Major Kane. If you had seen the men it would be a different matter.'

'I wondered if it could have been those men you were telling me about,' suggested Mac. 'I mean the men who were staying at Raddles' Inn. You said you didn't like the look of them?'

'Neether I do.'

'Are they still hanging about the village?'

'They are indeed. They are here now, in the Public Bar. Would you care to take a wee peep at them, Mac?'

This was by no means the first time that Mac had been invited to take a wee peep of the Public Bar so without more ado he sprang on to a chair, slid back a piece of wood and placed his eye to a small round hole in the panelling. It was an old device – few people knew of it – but Mac found it fascinating for from this vantage point you could see and not be seen. (It occurred to Mac that the old peep-hole was the reason why Jamie MacTaggart knew everything that went on in Ardfalloch.)

The Public Bar was full of men, as it always was at this time of day, but they were all local men – except two – so it was easy for Mac to identify the strangers. He had expected to see a couple of villains but these men looked harmless enough. In fact they looked quite peaceful and pleasant. They were standing at the bar-counter drinking beer and talking to each other: one was tall and thin with long legs and a sallow complexion, the other was shorter and stockily built with a round red face and bushy eyebrows. Both were tidily dressed in shirts and slacks and cardigan jackets (the sort of garments one can buy 'off the peg' in any shop which caters for men's requirements).

Mac gazed at them with interest . . . but it was quite impossible to decide whether or not these were the two shadowy figures he had seen in the fog. He replaced the small piece of wood and came down.

'Are they the ones?' asked MacTaggart eagerly.

'I don't know,' said Mac. 'They look quite harmless to me. Why are you worried about them?'

'They are different,' MacTaggart explained. 'In Ardfalloch we are used to gentlemen for the fishing, and shepherds and such-like, and chaps from the aluminium works, but these men are different. If you were seeing them in Glasgow – or any big town – you would not be surprised. It is just that I like to know who people are and what they are doing . . . and I would like to know where they get their money.'

'Perhaps they're just having a holiday.'

'Well, maybe,' agreed MacTaggart in doubtful tones. 'Maybe that's the way of it but it seems to me that they are not the sort that would be taking their holidays in Ardfalloch.'

'You said they were making trouble in the village. What are they doing?'

'They have a big shiny car and their pockets are full of money so they are taking girls over to Kincraig to see the pictures. Maybe you will laugh, Mac, but it is not very funny.'

In spite of his 'keen sense of humour' Mac did not feel inclined to laugh. Obviously it was pretty sickening for the lads of the village to have their girl-friends snatched from beneath their noses and whirled away in a big shiny car to the cinemas in Kincraig.

'Maybe you are thinking I am a foolish old busybody,' said MacTaggart. 'But I am not liking it. No, I am not liking it at all – and Mistress MacTaggart feels the same as me. Time was when you could speak to a lassie for her own good but nowadays they laugh at you. There's not one of them will take a telling.'

'I don't think you're a busybody,' replied Mac, patting his old friend on the shoulder. 'I think you're a very useful man, but it's no good my ringing up Major Kane and telling him—'

'That is what I said,' interrupted MacTaggart. 'I told you it would be a pity to bother Major Kane. I will keep my eyes open and maybe in a day or two we will find something else to tell him.'

It was on this somewhat mournful note that they parted.

Mac had hoped that Jamie MacTaggart would have been
able to throw more light on the problem so he was disappointed. He had a curiously strong inclination to ring up
Major Kane and ask his advice . . . but what could he say?
It was all too vague. He had been very upset at the time but
now the attack in the Pass was fading from his mind like
a bad dream – it would have been quite different if Colin
had been seriously injured.

Thus thinking Mac got one or two things from Mrs
Grant, called at the post office for the letters and went home.

There was a big sheaf of letters; most of them were for
Oliver of course but one of them was for Gerald from Sir
Walter MacCallum. Gerald was pleased when he saw it: he
had been expecting a letter for days. It was a large bulky
envelope so he took it up to his room to read in peace. He
sat down on the window-seat and opened it.

The first part of the letter was concerned with business
matters: with news about the ship which had been built
for a firm in Hamburg: her trials had been successfully
completed and except for a few small adjustments she was
ready. (Gerald had helped with the electrical equipment of
the ship when he first went to MacCallum's Yard.)

Sir Walter went on to say that the security measures at
the Yard had been altered and instead of the wires below the
surface which set off the alarm bells an entirely new system
had been installed. It was more satisfactory in every way.
Sir Walter seemed to think that the new system had been
'invented' by Gerald and complimented him on his in-
genuity.

Gerald smiled when he read this. He had not 'invented' it
of course but had merely adapted it from a radar device
which was used on main roads for testing the speed of cars.
Gerald had shown his plan to Mr Carr, the chief electrical
engineer at MacCallum's, but Mr Carr had refused to

consider it. Apparently Mr Carr had changed his mind! Sir
Walter continued:

'A funny thing happened last Sunday night, I went down
to the Yard after dinner – as I often do – and I was
prowling about in a leisurely way when suddenly all the
alarm bells in the place went off with a frightful racket.
Carr said I had broken the circuit – whatever that means!
It was quite a good thing to happen as it gave the
night-watchmen a fright and a chance to show their
mettle. In less than five minutes the lights had been
turned on and the whole place was full of men with
guard-dogs. I don't mind telling you I felt rather ashamed
of myself but everybody seemed to think I had done it on
purpose and we all congratulated each other on a successful rehearsal. Joseph Parker has been busy snooping but
has not found much wrong in "MacCallum's". However
he says I am to warn you about some men who were
involved in the robbery at K. and K's. Parker is certain
that they belonged to the gang but they escaped capture.
He says they have "gone north" – they were making for
Inverness – but I don't think you need take the warning
seriously. I fail to see how they could find you (you
are well-hidden at the House of the Deer). And why
should they want to get in touch with you? It is much
more likely that they are looking for jobs in the aluminium
works.

Please thank Mac for the venison. It was excellent eating. I enclose a letter from Bess – her usual style!

We are all well and send our love and best wishes for
good sport.

Yours ever

Walter.'

The letter from Bess in 'her usual style' consisted of a brief message on a large sheet of paper saying that she and Margaret were flourishing and sent love and kisses.

When Gerald had read the letter he went to find Mac and discovered him in the gun-room, sitting at the table doing nothing. He looked dejected.

'Hullo, what's the matter?' asked Gerald.

'I've been thinking,' Mac replied. 'Monday was awful, wasn't it? I behaved like a perfect fool. The fact is I was frightened – it's no good denying it. First I was scared stiff because I thought the hummel was charging me and then I was scared by those thugs in the Pass. I had hold of that chap who attacked Colin and I let him go. I should have held on to him, but I thought Colin was dead. I lost my head completely. I don't know what would have happened if you hadn't been there. I don't think I'm a coward – not really. I mean if it had been a battle I'd have been prepared . . . but you don't expect things like that to happen on your own ground. It was all so uncanny. I expect you're absolutely fed up with me . . . and what Dad will think when he hears about it I simply don't know . . .'

This moaning was so unlike the usually cheerful Mac that Gerald was quite alarmed. 'Goodness, what nonsense!' he exclaimed. 'I'm not in the least fed up with you.'

'Well, I'm absolutely fed up with myself.'

'If you want the truth I thought you behaved extremely well in exceptionally difficult circumstances.'

'Did you really?'

'Yes, really, and I'm quite prepared to tell your father so – if that's what's worrying you.'

Apparently it was. Mac smiled wanly. 'But I don't want you to hide the truth,' he said. 'As a matter of fact I've been trying to write to Dad and tell him about it. That's what got me down. It wasn't until I had written the whole story that I realised what a juggins I had been.'

'You can't have written the true story,' said Gerald consolingly.

It took some time to comfort Mac . . . and, after that, it was a little difficult for Gerald to say what he had intended.

'Well, that's that,' said Gerald. 'We understand each other, don't we? Now I've got something to say to you: the mystery is solved.'

'The mystery is solved?'

'Yes. Here you are! Just read this letter from Sir Walter and you'll see for yourself.'

Mac took the letter and read it carefully. He said, 'But Gerald, I don't know anything about radar, so—'

'It isn't that,' interrupted Gerald. 'It's the next bit, about those men. I don't want to involve you in trouble so I had better make tracks. You understand, don't you?'

'I don't understand anything about it,' Mac declared.

'It was those men who attacked Colin in the Pass. Colin was walking beside you; he was wearing my coat and cap so they mistook him for me. When the cap fell off and they saw his hair they realised their mistake and fled for their lives. That explains everything, doesn't it?'

For a minute or two Mac was silent, thinking about it. Then he said, 'Yes, I suppose it does, but what was their object? Why did they want to kill you?'

'They didn't want to kill me: it wasn't a killing blow. They just wanted to stun me and take me away and ask me a few questions.'

'Questions about what?'

'About the security measures in MacCallum's Shipyard.'

'I still don't understand,' said Mac, hopelessly.

Gerald saw that he would have to explain the matter more fully if he wanted Mac to understand . . . so he explained it from beginning to end.

'But all this has nothing to do with you,' added Gerald. 'The point is I don't want to involve you in my troubles.

They're sure to have another try so I had better leave here early tomorrow morning.'

'No!' cried Mac. 'No, that's rot! Why should you? To begin with I'm not sure you're right – it seems fantastic to me – and even if it *was* those men who attacked Colin, thinking it was you, and even if they *did* have another try to kidnap you (or whatever you think they're going to do). Well, we shall have something to say to that! There are three of us – four, counting Malcolm – so we'll give them a run for their money.'

'Mac, listen, they may come here—'

'I hope they do! It will be fun!'

'It won't be fun,' said Gerald gravely. 'It might be very serious trouble. Those men will stick at nothing. They're dangerous.'

'Dangerous?' echoed Mac incredulously. 'The two men I saw at MacTaggart's didn't look dangerous.'

'They may not look it but they are. The chief of the gang is "a ruthless devil". That's what Sir Walter said about him . . . and the girls are here. We've got to think of the girls.'

'Yes . . . well . . . what do you propose to do?'

'Nothing very heroic,' replied Gerald, smiling. 'I shall leave here early and go down to the village and ring up your friend, Major Kane. I can do it from MacTaggart's Inn . . .'

'I'll come with you.'

'No, you'll stay here and look after the girls.'

'If it's still misty you'll get lost.'

'I shan't get lost. I know the place pretty well by this time. I shall go by the short cut and the stepping-stones. They may be watching the bridge.'

Mac was frowning. He said, 'I don't like it. Honestly, Gerald, it will be much better if I come with you . . .'

'No,' said Gerald firmly. He had argued with Mac before – and had given in – but this time he stuck to his guns.

'Oh, all right,' said Mac at last. 'Have it your own way . . . but I shall get up early and see you off. I'll let you out by a little window in the cellar, in case they're watching the doors.'

23 Describes a man-hunt over the hills

Gerald wakened early and saw that it was still misty. He dressed quickly in his stalking clothes and went into Mac's room. He, too, was up and dressed.

They went down to the kitchen together and Mac led the way to a trap-door with a ladder leading down to the cellar. It was a big old-fashioned cellar which stretched the full length of the house, low in the roof and vaulted like a crypt. The wine-bins were empty but there was a pile of empty bottles in one corner. Gerald looked round the place with interest.

'By Jove, your ancestors did themselves well!' he exclaimed.

'Yes, there was a good deal of contraband trade with France in the old days. My great-great-grandfather used to have parties here. I expect he was mixed up with smugglers. We really ought to get these bottles cleared out—'

'Don't chuck them away,' interrupted Gerald. 'Most of these bottles are hand-made and quite valuable nowadays.'

While they were talking Mac had opened a small square window at the far end of the cellar. He had used the window when he was a boy as a secret entrance to Tigh na Feidh. He was surprised to find how small it was!

'Do you think you can get through?' he asked doubtfully.

Gerald thought he could. It was a tight fit but by dint of pushing and squeezing he managed it and found himself in a thick shrubbery of rhododendron bushes.

'Be careful,' said Mac anxiously.

'Oh yes! I'll be all right.'

'What are you going to do after you've phoned? You'll come straight back here, won't you?'

Gerald had not considered this point. He said, 'I'll take Major Kane's advice. You said he was good value, didn't you?'

'Yes, I liked him immensely.'

The two friends said goodbye; Mac shut the little window and Gerald started off. It was damp and cold and misty but he was quite pleased about the mist: if those men were lurking about it would be easier for him to avoid them.

Gerald ran down the steep path which led to the plantation of pine trees . . . and then stopped! Somebody had closed the gate with a loud click and there was a crunching sound of heavy boots coming up the path towards him. He hesitated, wondering if he should hide and let them pass, and then he decided on a better plan. It sprang into his mind all of a sudden! If he let them pass they would go up to the house, thinking he was there. They might be dangerous (he had told Mac they were dangerous men). Gerald did not really believe they were dangerous – except perhaps to himself – but Phil and Donny were in the house and, at the very least, they would be a nuisance. They might hang about all day at the house, waiting for him to come out.

All this passed through his mind in a flash and he saw what he would do. He would lead them away from the house and lose them on the hill. It would not be difficult for he knew his way. The mist, though not very thick, was thick enough to hide him. Then, when he had thrown off his pursuers, he could drop down to the river and phone from MacTaggart's Inn as he had intended.

He shouted, 'Hullo, who's there? What do you want?'

The footsteps stopped and for a few moments there was silence. Then a voice replied, 'We want to speak to Mr Burleigh Brown.'

'All right! Here I am!' shouted Gerald. He added, 'Come and get me.' Then he turned and ran.

The ruse succeeded. He heard them coming after him and made for the rock where he and Mac usually met Malcolm and the boy with the pony. He left the path, crossed the little burn by the stepping-stones and took to the heather.

He heard them crossing the burn, splashing in the water and cursing heartily, but instead of keeping on up the path they came after him up the hill and he realised that he was leaving an easily defined track in the wet heather, so he turned left on to the bare hillside and increased his pace. He was not really afraid of being caught for after ten days of stalking he was in good training and it was most unlikely that his pursuers could keep up the pace for long.

At first they kept on shouting to him to stop, assuring him that all they wanted was to talk to him for a few minutes, but when they saw that he had no intention of stopping they ceased to shout and came on in grim silence. Probably they needed all their breath for climbing.

The mist became thinner as Gerald climbed upwards for there was a stirring of air which lifted it and sent it whirling gently like smoke. He could now see all round him for about twenty steps, beyond that the mist was like a white wall. Gerald began to get a little worried for if the mist became too thin they would see him and it was just possible that they had a rifle with them! If so would they shoot – or not?

It was then that Gerald saw a stunted rowan tree (he had noticed it when he had been for his solitary walk on Sunday and it had impressed him because of its strange shape) and he realised that he was approaching the 'queer' part of Ard na Feidh, so he struck off his previous course at an angle and climbed on faster than before. He had hoped to shake off his pursuers, but it was impossible to

climb fast without dislodging loose stones which rolled
downhill and betrayed his whereabouts.

Gerald was in the 'queer' part of the forest now with
the rocks and bogs and stunted rowans. He came over a
ridge and saw that at the bottom of the declivity there was
a pool of slimy green water; it might have been the very
same bog which had given him such a fright on Sunday or
it might have been another. It looked the same. He ran
round the edge of it as fast as he could and then stopped and
looked back: two shadowy figures, one tall and lanky, the
other shorter and thick-set, emerged from the surrounding
mist.

'There he is!' shouted the tall one. With that they came
towards him; next moment they were both stuck firmly in
the mud.

Gerald left them there struggling and cursing and ran
down the hill. He had lost his bearings by this time but he
found a burn and followed it – all the burns on this side of
the forest drained into the river – and before long he found
the wire fence and the creaky gate.

Once or twice during the mad chase Gerald had been a bit
frightened. He was too imaginative not to realise that
various things might happen: the mist might lift or he
might fall and hurt himself, he might sprain his ankle, but
now that he had eluded his pursuers and left them flounder-
ing in the bog he had lost all fear of them.

All morning he had been too engrossed in avoiding capture to have had time to think about what he was going to
say to Major Kane. He must tell him everything of course
but really there was not much to tell. He had not seen his
pursuers except as two shadowy figures in the mist. How
much better it would be if he could identify them!

He had got to this point in his reflections when he heard
the click of the gate in the wire fence at the top of the

plantation (it was a loud creak, a sort of grinding sound, so there was no mistaking it) and he realised that the two men must have managed to extricate themselves from the bog and were still in pursuit.

What should he do? There would be time to run on to the stepping-stones and cross the river to the road . . . but then, quite suddenly, he remembered a Red Indian trick (he had been an avid reader of Fenimore Cooper when he was a boy) and here was an ideal place to employ it . . . so he walked down to the river in the wet mud and then stepped backwards, putting his feet carefully in the same footprints. Then he swung himself up into the nearest oak, an ancient giant, and settled himself amongst its branches. That would give them something to think about, thought Gerald, smiling to himself.

A few minutes later the long lanky man came running down the path. He looked at the footprints, crossed the river by the stepping-stones and came back. Meanwhile the second man had come down the path. He was gasping like a fish. He threw himself on the ground.

'I'm done,' he declared. 'I'm not going a step farther – not till I have a rest. Besides you don't know that he's come this way—'

'Yes, I do,' interrupted the tall lanky man. 'Oh, it was luck, I grant you that. I had a hunch that he was on his way to get his car and bunk when we met him this morning, so I thought he would have another try. Then it was easy enough to pick up his spoor at the gate. The soles of his rubber boots are an unusual pattern. He's come this way all right.'

'Oh well, he's across the river and on the road by this time, so—'

'He didn't cross the river.'

'What d'you mean? Those are his footprints, aren't they?'

'Yes, but there aren't any prints on the other side.'

'Where is he, then?'

'In the river – unless he has wings, of course.'

'How d'you mean, "in the river"?'

'It's an old dodge. He's wading in the water.'

'Has he gone up or down?'

'How do I know?'

'You're supposed to be tracking him.'

'A man doesn't leave footprints in running water. We had better separate. You can go up the river and I'll go down.'

'Nothing doing.'

'What do you mean? He's only a few minutes ahead of us. Come on, Grooby! We'll get him if we hurry.'

'I'm not going after him alone. That's flat.'

'Spinner will be furious if we lose him again.'

'Let him be furious. I'm just about sick of Spinner. Why does he want this fellow so badly?'

They were both sitting down now, just beneath the tree but the foliage was so thick that Gerald could not see them properly. He could see their feet. He could smell the smoke from the cigarettes they had lighted and he could hear their voices quite clearly but their voices were just like thousands of other voices. Neither of the men had any identifiable accent.

'Why does he want this fellow so badly?' repeated the man called Grooby in a lower tone.

'He doesn't tell me his secrets,' was the reply. 'As a matter of fact it's better to do as you're told and not ask questions. Spinner isn't a patient man.'

'Have you ever seen Spinner?'

'I saw him this morning.'

'Do you mean he's here?'

'Yes, at the Inn – but he's not liking it much. It's a foul hole, isn't it?'

'The new wing isn't so bad. I mean the new wing where

we have our meals – but the old part of the house is full of dry rot and wood-worm. I know a bit about old houses (I was in the building trade at one time) so Raddle was talking to me about it, asking what he could do to the place. I told him the best thing he could do was to burn it.'

There was a short silence, then Grooby rolled over on to his stomach and groaned. 'Oh hell, I'm stiff and sore!' he complained. 'I'm not used to climbing hills like you . . .'

Gerald could see him better now. He could see the greasy hair straggling over his collar and sticking out ears.

'You'll be stiffer tomorrow,' said his companion unfeelingly.

'It's not good enough,' Grooby declared. 'We do the work and take the risk – and what do we get out of it? What did you get out of the dockyard affair?'

'That's not your business.'

'All right. Don't get shirty. You got the same as me, I suppose. I just meant what does he get out of it. He takes good care of himself and rakes in the money.'

'He's clever,' objected the thin man. 'You've got to have a planner to organise these affairs.'

'It's not good enough,' Grooby repeated. 'I want to get out of the racket.'

The thin man laughed. (It was not a pleasant sound.) He said, 'Nobody gets out of this racket and stays alive.'

'Rushton got out.'

'Yes, Rushton got out – and what happened to him?'

'You mean it wasn't an accident?'

'How do I know? All I say is: it was a lucky accident for Spinner . . . and I suppose you think it was an accident that Fison fell out of a top-floor window? And what about Harry Brown? Harry was on his way to Rome when his plane exploded in the air. Funny all these "accidents", don't you think?'

'I liked Harry,' said Grooby reflectively. 'He was a decent sort. If I thought Spinner had done for Harry I'd put a bullet through him – that's what.'

'You wouldn't dare.'

'I would.'

There was a short silence. Then Grooby spoke again. He said, 'As a matter of fact that might be the best way . . .'

'Well, don't tell me about it. I don't want to know your plans. See?'

'I've no plans,' declared Grooby. 'I just meant—'

'Be quiet!'

'Why? What's the trouble?'

'I heard something!'

The fat man sat up and looked round uneasily. 'What did you hear?' he asked.

For a moment Gerald was alarmed: he had moved his foot slightly and one of the old dry twigs had snapped.

'Oh, nothing much,' replied the thin man carelessly. 'Must have been a rabbit or something.' He rose and added, 'Come on! You've had your rest. We'll have one more try – and then go back to the Horseman's Inn for a meal.'

'What's the good? You said you didn't know which way he'd gone?'

'I've a hunch he's gone up the river.'

'You and your hunches!'

'I was right last time, wasn't I?'

Grooby got up and straightened his back – and groaned.

'Come on,' said his companion impatiently.

They set off together on their wild goose chase.

Gerald saw them go. They were following the path up the river and talking as they went. It struck him that if they really expected to find him it would have been more sensible to be silent . . . but that was their look-out.

Gerald was pleased with himself: he had led them up

hill and down dale and finally he had outwitted them. He
decided to give them five minutes to get well on their
way, then he would climb down from his hiding-place and
run as fast as he could in the opposite direction. He would
make for the hump-backed bridge; from thence it would be
easy to get to MacTaggart's and ring up the police.

Gerald waited for five minutes. Then he climbed down
and jumped. He landed lightly on his feet and was about to
set off on the last lap of his run when the two men sprang
upon him and seized him. A sack was pulled over his head
and tied tightly round his knees and he was flung to the
ground. He struggled and tried to shout but he was helpless. The next moment he felt a sharp stab in his thigh – like
the sting of a wasp – and realised that he had been doped.
As he drifted into unconsciousness he heard his captors
laughing. It was not a pleasant sound.

24   In which is recorded Gerald's adventures at the Horseman's Inn

When Gerald came to himself he discovered that he was lying on a settee in a room that he had never seen before. His ankles were tied together and his arms were bound to his body so that he could not move hand nor foot. At first his brain was dazed but gradually he recovered and remembered what had happened . . . and cursed himself for his folly! He had been too pleased with himself. He had underestimated his enemies and had been trapped like a silly rabbit!

The room was large and old and very dirty with oak panelling on the walls and ragged curtains at the open window. Gerald could see the tops of trees: their leaves were moving gently in the evening breeze. He had just decided that this must be the old part of Raddles' Inn when the door opened and three men appeared. Two of them were the men who had captured Gerald (the tall thin individual and the short fat man). The third man was clean and well-dressed in a brown tweed suit and was wearing large dark spectacles. He gave orders that the prisoner was to be lifted and placed in a wooden chair with arms which stood beside a table in the middle of the room. His ankles were loosened and his feet were tied to the legs of the chair in a very uncomfortable position.

'Is that right, sir—' asked the thin man.

'He's still fuddled,' was the reply. 'Bring a large cup of coffee and loosen his arms. You must have given him too much dope.'

'It was the only way we could get him. He was fighting-mad.'

'I don't want excuses. Do as you're told and hurry up about it, Lanky.'

'Lanky' carried out the orders without another word.

So this was the Spinner, thought Gerald. This was the head of the gang! Gerald wished he could tear off the spectacles and see what the man looked like. (Walter had said he was a genius in his own line of country!)

Gerald's mouth was dry – his tongue felt like a piece of leather – so he was glad to see the cup of steaming coffee. He realised that there might be more dope in it but he thought it unlikely. He thought the Spinner wanted to question him. He was right of course: his two captors were dismissed in a summary fashion; the Spinner locked the door and sat down opposite Gerald at the table.

'I want to talk to you,' he said. 'I'm sorry it had to be like this, but there was no other way. The dope they gave you is harmless: you'll feel better when you've had some coffee. Don't try any tricks. I've got a revolver in my pocket but I have no intention of using it if you behave sensibly. All I want is information. If your information is useful I'm willing to pay you a good price for it.'

'What do you want?'

'I want a little information about the security measures in MacCallum's Shipyard. I know a good deal already: for instance I know about the baker's van. It was quite a clever dodge, but not quite clever enough: a man at the garage tried to move it and found it unexpectedly heavy (it's bullet-proof of course). I paid him handsomely for that information and gave him a passport and his fare to Australia. He's well on his way by this time. I'll do the same for you.'

Gerald was silent. He was drinking the coffee (it was

good, well-made coffee, hot and strong and sweet) and his brain was clearing.

'Come now,' said the Spinner persuasively. 'All I want from you is some information about the alarm signals. They are worked by electric wires which run beneath the surface of the ground. They start up the bells and turn on the lights. I want to know exactly where they are hidden. When you have given me the information you can walk out of here, a free man with a thousand pounds in your pocket – a thousand pounds, a passport and a ticket to any place in the world – or you can go back to your job at MacCallum's if you prefer it.'

'What do you mean?'

'Nobody will know about our little arrangement except you and me. You will be the richer by a thousand pounds.'

'Why ask me?'

'Because you're an electrician. I expect you helped to lay the wires so you know all about them.'

This was true: Gerald had helped to instal the cables so he knew exactly where they had been hidden. He also knew that quite recently they had been removed and replaced by the radar device. The information that the Spinner wanted was worthless: it didn't matter whether he gave it or not.

Gerald thought about it seriously: should he give this man the information? Meanwhile he played for time. 'It's too little for such a big risk,' he said sulkily.

'Two thousand, then?' suggested the Spinner. 'I've got a chart of the Yard and a red pencil. All you have to do is to trace the course of the wires – it won't take you ten minutes. Then you can leave here, a free man. You can go abroad or you can go back to your job and forget all about our little piece of business. I shan't bother you any more.'

'Supposing I refuse?'

'That would be foolish. It would mean I should have to send you to Mr Spinner to deal with. He has ways and means of making people talk. Sometimes, if people refuse to carry out his orders, he's a little rough. You wouldn't like that, would you?'

'I thought you were the Spinner.'

'Dear me, no! Mr Spinner leaves all this sort of business to me. I wonder what gave you the idea that I was Mr Spinner.'

There was something in the man's demeanour which confirmed Gerald's conviction that this was the Spinner himself. He was certain of it. This was the man who planned the raids and the robberies and watched from a safe distance while his underlings carried out orders. This was the 'ruthless devil' who had eliminated Rushton and Fison and Harry Bown – and probably half a dozen others – when they ceased to be of any use to him. They knew too much so he couldn't afford to let them go and he had taken steps to silence them for ever. Gerald realised that he was in the same boat! He knew too much. Therefore it was better, for his own sake, to pretend that the information he possessed was valuable and to refuse to give it. Then, perhaps, the Spinner would keep him alive for a few days longer and he might have a chance to escape.

It was pretty hopeless: he saw that. The mere fact that the bribe was so large and had been doubled without the slightest hesitation showed that the Spinner had no intention of handing over the money. There would be another 'regrettable accident' and this time Gerald Burleigh Brown would be the victim.

Curiously enough Gerald wasn't frightened. He was surprised at this, himself. Perhaps it was because it was all so extraordinary that he couldn't believe it was real . . . or perhaps he was still slightly under the influence of the dope they had given him.

'Come on,' said the Spinner impatiently. 'Make up your mind. I can't wait here all night.'

'Well, I don't know,' replied Gerald in doubtful tones. 'I've got a good, well-paid job and I shouldn't like to lose it. Two thousand pounds is a lot of money, but it wouldn't last for ever. I can't make up my mind in a hurry.'

The Spinner hesitated for a moment and then took a large envelope from his pocket and produced a map. 'Very well,' he said. 'You can have half an hour. Look, here's the map!'

Gerald watched while the Spinner spread the map on the table and smoothed out the creases . . . and was reminded of Malcolm who had done the same thing with his map of Ard na Feidh! But whereas Malcolm's map was a rough and ready sketch, this map was a professional chart, drawn to scale, and whereas Malcolm's hands were the hands of a worker – big and hard and brown – this man's hands were as smooth and white as the hands of a woman. There was something queer about these hands. Something that Gerald found rather disgusting.

'It's a good map, isn't it?' said the map-maker. 'I see you find it interesting. Map-making is one of my hobbies.'

Gerald found the map a little too 'interesting'. It was correct in every detail. He wondered how the Spinner had obtained all his information.

'You must have been there yourself!' exclaimed Gerald.

'Oh yes! I have ways and means of getting into the place whenever I feel inclined. Bolts and bars and guard-dogs (and all the other silly devices) are useless to keep me out of any place when I make up my mind to get in.' He laughed and added, 'And the police know to their cost that bolts and bars are useless to keep me in if I want to get out.'

He was mad, of course! The Spinner was a megalomaniac – like Napoleon and Hitler and all the other men who had wielded absolute power. For the first time Gerald was a little frightened.

'What do you want?' he asked.

'I've told you. I want you to study the map and draw the course of the wires with a red pencil.'

'You want more than that.'

'Well, perhaps,' agreed the Spinner. 'But we'll start with the wires. When you've done that – and done it correctly – I may ask you a few questions. Oh, nothing important, of course! You needn't be alarmed. I promise you faithfully that if you behave sensibly you shall be a free man in half an hour.'

'You must give me more time—'

'More time for what?' interrupted the Spinner. 'Don't you realise your position? You're a helpless prisoner. I can do as I like with you. I can lock you up in the cellar and starve you, or I can give you some other unpleasant treatment. This wretched hovel is miles off the beaten track – that's why I chose it for my temporary headquarters – so you can shout and yell as loud as you like; nobody will hear you. I've got four of my own men here and the Raddles are in my pocket. That's your position, *Mister Burleigh Brown*.'

Suddenly Gerald was angry: too angry to continue the farce!

'You can have your answer now,' he declared . . . and, with that, he seized the map, tore it to bits and threw the pieces into a waste-paper basket which was standing under the table.

'How silly!' exclaimed the Spinner furiously. 'You don't suppose that's my original map, do you? This was only a copy. You're a bit too uppish, *Mister Burleigh Brown*! Perhaps you don't understand plain English! Perhaps you think I don't mean what I say? Perhaps a little psychological treatment is what you need: it may teach you better manners . . .' He took a cord, tied Gerald's hands behind his back and then paused. 'But I mustn't be too rough,' he added softly.

The first blow landed upon the prisoner's right eye, the

second on his left eyebrow. After that there was a succession of blows, first on one ear and then on the other. They were not very hard, but they sent his head swinging from side to side and made his ears buzz like a swarm of angry bees.

The brutal attack was so sudden and unexpected that Gerald almost fainted. It was not so much the pain (though that was bad enough) it was the absolute helplessness which was so unbearable. He had known that he was a helpless prisoner but the treatment he was receiving brought it home to him: he couldn't raise a finger to defend himself; he couldn't even wipe away the blood which was running down his face from a cut in his eyebrow.

'There, that will do in the meantime,' said the Spinner. 'It's just a little foretaste of what you'll get if you're unreasonable. Not very pleasant, is it?'

The Spinner didn't wait for an answer. He turned and went away, locking the door behind him.

Gerald was too dazed to think. Then when his senses returned, he remembered reading about the treatment given to prisoners in Nazi Camps during the war: they had been tied up and battered. The treatment was given daily by men who had been trained in psychology and knew how to graduate the punishment. Each 'treatment' had been a little more violent until at the end of a week the wretched prisoner's spirit was broken! Gerald saw that it could easily be true. For a while he remained inert, slumped in the chair trying to regain some measure of courage . . .

Then suddenly he sat up and gazed about him. There was a strange smell in the room! What was it? Where did it come from? Little spirals of smoke were rising from the cracks between the ill-fitting boards of the old oaken floor! They wavered in the still air and drifted, forming a thin cloud which rose to the ceiling.

Smoke! The place was on fire! Nothing could have

revived the prisoner more quickly. He struggled to loosen the cords which bound his hands and feet – but the man who had bound him had known his job: the knots were secure; the cords too strong to break.

Somebody had said that the old part of The Horseman's Inn was full of wood-worm and dry rot and the best thing to do was to burn it. Who had said that? It was Grooby, of course! Perhaps Raddle had taken Grooby's advice . . . or (even more horrifying!) perhaps the Spinner himself had set fire to the place! It would be another 'regrettable accident' like the explosion in the plane when Harry Brown was on his way to Rome.

'Fire!' shouted Gerald. 'Fire! Help! Help! The house is on fire!'

It was useless to shout for help if Raddle or the Spinner had set fire to the place on purpose but Gerald's instinct was to shout so he kept on shouting until he was hoarse and the smoke caught the back of his throat and made him cough. He was still shouting and struggling and coughing – and his ears were still buzzing – when a hand was laid on his shoulder and a voice said, 'Be quiet! It's a friend. It's Shipman's guttersnipe.'

The cords which bound his feet and hands had been tied so firmly that even when they had been cut he couldn't move . . . but strong arms lifted him from the chair, carried him across the room and dropped him out of the window (strong arms which certainly didn't belong to 'Shipman's guttersnipe'). He fell softly into a stretched-out blanket and was picked up and bundled into the back seat of a waiting car.

It was very dark by this time – dark and misty and smoky – but there were people about: quite a crowd of men, moving hither and thither, talking in low voices. Some of them were carrying old-fashioned stable lanterns, others had electric torches. The lights were twinkling on brass helmets and on the shiny black peaks of policeman's hats. It was a weird scene: it was like a scene in a play; it was all the more strange because, although Gerald could hear the murmur of innumerable voices, he couldn't understand a word they were saying. Where had he got to? What was happening?

Then, suddenly, a hand was laid firmly on his knee and a well-known voice said clearly, 'You are all right, Mister Gerald. There is no need for you to worry. I am here with the Ardfalloch Fire Brigade . . . and Major Kane is here with the policemen from Kincraig. Look, I will tuck this blanket round you and you can have a wee sleep. There, that is better. You are warm and comfortable now.'

Gerald couldn't reply. His rescue had happened so suddenly and unexpectedly that he could scarcely believe it was real. Perhaps he was dreaming. Perhaps he would wake to find himself still a prisoner in a smoke-filled room, tied to a wooden chair!

'Oh, there you are, MacTaggart!' exclaimed another voice, (the crisp, clear voice of a man, used to command). 'I was looking for you. How many men have you got?'

'There are six of us, sir. Some of the lads are busy getting the engine started and laying the hose. It is not a very good engine but Euan knows the way of it.'

'Is Mr Burleigh Brown all right?'

'He is not bad at all, Major. I have him safe—'

'It was a neat job, MacTaggart!'

'Och, it was nothing,' declared the Big Fish modestly. He added, 'The lads are wanting to know if they can shoot. I was telling them we would need to get your permission—'

'Shoot?' exclaimed Major Kane. 'Good heavens! Are they carrying fire-arms?'

'Not fire-arms,' said MacTaggart hastily. 'Not fire-arms, Major. Some of them have wee pistols . . . just mementoes, Major. Just wee mementoes over from the war.'

'And how do you suppose I can account for a body with a bullet in it?' inquired Major Kane. 'No, MacTaggart, I can't give them permission to use revolvers. Tell them that, will you?' He had scarcely spoken when there was a loud report, followed almost immediately by two more.

'Good lord!' ejaculated Major Kane.

'It iss not uss, sir,' declared a soft Highland voice. 'It iss them, shooting each other. It iss a chentleman in a prown coat, sir.'

'What do you mean, Dalgleish?'

'It wass one of his friends that hass shot him in the pack and kilt him – not uss, sir.'

Major Kane accepted this somewhat surprising statement calmly and proceeded to give orders to his sergeant, who had joined the little group that was standing near the car. 'We want them all, Sims,' said Major Kane. 'You had better station a man at every door and arrest them as they come out. The place is like a rabbit warren so it won't be easy. I wish I had brought twice the number of men – but Mr MacTaggart has six local lads who are willing to help.'

'Only too willing,' put in MacTaggart cheerfully. He added, 'Once they have got the fire under control I will tell them to report to you, Major.'

'The fire is under control, sir,' declared the sergeant. 'They got it in time to prevent it spreading. It was an electric wire in a lumber room that set fire to a dirty greasy old carpet. Mister Parker is of the opeenion that it was set fire to on purpose but there's no proof of that.'

'Better not mention it, then.'

'No, sir.'

'It's funny that nobody noticed it before. There's a hell of a lot of smoke.'

'That's true,' agreed Sims. 'But it's confined to the old part of the house. Everybody seems to be in the new part of the house having a meal. They've got enough whisky to float a battleship.'

'How do you know?'

'It was Mister Parker. He climbed up a tree and looked in at the window and saw them. There are no flies on Mister Parker. He says it's raw whisky they're drinking – foul stuff! It's my belief Raddle makes it himself.'

'Do you mean he has an illicit still?'

Sims nodded, 'But there's no proof of that either.'

'We can keep it in mind and look for it later. You had better get going, Sims. Tell our men to be as quiet as possible – we want to take them by surprise – there's sure to be a mad rush for the doors when they see the smoke.'

'Yes, sir, but it won't be all that difficult: most of them are half tight already.'

'I want them all, Sims. Everybody in the house.'

'Yes, sir.'

'They're dangerous. Don't forget that.'

'No, sir. We can – er – be a bit rough, I suppose?'

'As rough as you like, replied Major Kane cheerfully. He added, 'Meanwhile somebody must take Mr Burleigh Brown to the nearest hospital.'

'There is no need,' declared MacTaggart. 'He is sleeping now. I will take him to Katie.'

'Katie?'

'Katie MacTaggart. It is the wee white cottage by the bridge. Katie will see to him all right.'

25   In which an invalid receives visitors

Gerald did not waken until well on in the following day. He found himself in a small clean room with a coomceiled ceiling and a deerskin rug on the floor. He was trying to remember what had happened to him when Katie MacTaggart came in with a bowl of soup.

'Oh, you are better!' she exclaimed. 'You were unconscious when they carried you in last night and you looked so bad that I sent Colin for Doctor Wedderburn.'

'I can't remember what happened to me,' said Gerald frowning.

'Don't try to remember,' suggested his hostess. Just take the broth and go to sleep. Doctor Wedderburn gave you an injection and put three stitches in your eyebrow but he did it very neatly so the scar will soon disappear. He left some sedative tablets to help you to sleep and said he would look in and see you tomorrow.'

'I'm an awful nuisance,' Gerald murmured unhappily.

'Oh no!' replied Mrs MacTaggart. 'I am very pleased to look after you. I have had nursing experience, you know. I just wish I had a better room to give you: this is Sandy's room – and very small and bare. It is not what you have been used to at all! But Doctor Wedderburn wants you to keep quiet.' She shook up his pillows, gave him the soup and the tablets and settled him comfortably for the night.

Gerald was young and healthy so his cuts and bruises healed up quickly and the swelling went down, but it was not until the third day that he felt more like himself and began to remember things clearly. He explained this to the doctor.

'Don't worry,' said Doctor Wedderburn. 'It will take a few days for you to recover from the shock to your nervous system. The ear is a delicate piece of mechanism and closely connected with the brain . . . but it will soon come right. Just sleep as much as possible, that's the best treatment. Katie MacTaggart is a very good nurse: she'll look after you.'

'I want to know what happened,' Gerald told him.

'Well, you can see Mac if you like. He's here, asking for you, but I don't want you to get overtired.'

Gerald wanted to see Mac (no other visitor would have been more welcome) so Mac came in.

'Poor old chap!' exclaimed Mac. 'What a ghastly time you've had!'

'Oh, I'm better,' Gerald declared. 'Come and talk to me, Mac. I want to know what happened.'

'I should think you know more than I do about it!'

'At first I couldn't remember anything at all – which was horribly frightening – but now I'm beginning to remember. In fact I feel all right except for a headache. I've been lying here kicking myself for being such a fool. I was caught in a bag like a silly rabbit and rescued like a sack of potatoes.'

'I wasn't there . . . and anyway I'm not much good at explaining things. If you really want to know, you had better see Major Kane. He's very anxious to talk to you when you feel well enough. Could you bear it?'

Gerald said he could bear it, so the second visitor was conducted up the steep little flight of stairs and ushered into the room. Mac was tall but the second visitor was taller and a good deal broader so the room seemed overcrowded. It was obvious that Mrs MacTaggart didn't approve: she warned them not to overtire her patient and went away.

'I shan't stay long,' said Major Kane. 'I've got my prisoners safely locked up and Scotland Yard is sending guards to take them to London but I shall have to write a report so I'll be glad of any information you can give me. You've got very good friends, Mr Burleigh Brown, especially James MacTaggart. If it hadn't been for him we wouldn't have been able to find you. It was he who rang me up and told me that you had been kidnapped by two men and were a prisoner at The Horseman's Inn.'

'How did he know?'

'He didn't tell me – as a matter of fact I didn't ask – he was very upset about you. He was quite frantic. So I agreed to take some of my men and rescue you without delay. I didn't expect much trouble – certainly not a pitched battle – so I hadn't brought nearly enough police to deal with the situation. I was wondering what on earth to do when MacTaggart himself turned up with the Arfalloch Fire Brigade.'

Mac said thoughtfully: 'I've sometimes wondered if a private Fire Brigade is legal.'

'I don't know – and I don't want to know,' replied the Chief Constable. 'I can see snags of course. It might cause jealousy and muddle if they interfered with an official fire-fighting force but, under the leadership of a man like MacTaggart, I'm all for it. (I should hate to have to disband the Ardfalloch Fire Brigade so we'll just keep dark about it, shall we?) Anyhow it arrived in the nick of time: five brawny Highlanders wearing brass helmets, like old-fashioned coal scuttles, and an insignificant little fellow in plain clothes. They looked like something out of *The Pirates of Penzance* – but I can tell you I was pleased to see them! (A band of angels straight from heaven couldn't have been more welcome!) and the insignificant little fellow is worth his weight in gold.'

'Joseph Parker,' murmured Gerald.

'Yes, that's the chap. It was he who heard you shouting and found a ladder in the stables . . . and he was first up the ladder, as nimbly as a monkey, with the blacksmith's son close behind. Meanwhile MacTaggart and Co. had organised a stretched blanket to catch you. The rescue was carried out smartly and efficiently. A professional brigade couldn't have done it better.'

'Did they put out the fire?' Gerald wanted to know.

'It wasn't a serious fire – just a greasy old carpet. My fellows had found it and extinguished it before the Ardfalloch lads arrived.' Major Kane smiled and added, 'They were a bit disappointed: they had hoped for "a real good blaze".'

'There was a lot of smoke,' said Gerald.

'Yes, I know. Your friend, Parker, thinks there was something fishy about it: he says the carpet was impregnated with a chemical which caused it to smoulder for hours – but I'm not a chemist so I don't know about that – and anyhow there are enough puzzles in this case without mentioning arson.'

'Was anybody injured?' asked Mac.

'One of the prisoners is dead: somebody shot him through the heart.'

There was a short silence.

Major Kane continued: 'The police weren't armed, of course, but some of the local lads were armed. MacTaggart said they had wee pistols: "just mementoes over from the war". None of the "wee pistols" had been discharged so I'm keeping quiet about it. If I were to mention that some of them had revolvers in their pockets I should have to take measures against them for carrying fire-arms.'

Gerald had been listening with interest: the pieces of the puzzle were taking shape. He said quietly, 'I've no proof of course – so perhaps it isn't much use – but I shouldn't be surprised to hear that the Spinner was killed by one of his own gang.'

'What!' exclaimed Major Kane. 'Good heavens! Please tell me exactly what happened.'

Gerald told him. The chase over the hills could be told in a few words but the conversation between 'Lanky' and Grooby took longer and was more difficult to remember in detail. Finally he reported his conversation with the Spinner. Major Kane listened carefully and then said: 'You heard Grooby threaten to put a bullet through Spinner? Sometimes people make threats and don't really mean to carry them out.'

'Grooby meant it,' replied Gerald with conviction. 'Grooby wants to "get out of the racket".'

'So you really think he carried out his intention and that the man who questioned you was Spinner himself?'

'Yes, I'm almost certain he was the head of the gang. I couldn't swear to it, of course. He pretended he wasn't the Spinner but he spoke as if he had complete authority and offered me two thousand pounds for the information he wanted.'

'Two thousand!' echoed Mac in amazement.

'Oh, he didn't intend to give me the money! He just meant to get the information out of me. Then, when he had got what he wanted and I was of no further use to him, he would have put an end to me. There would have been another "regrettable accident"—'

'But you would have been of use to him,' interrupted the Major. 'You underrate Spinner. He lays his plans with a view to the future. If you had accepted the bribe you would have been in his power for the rest of your life. That's the way he gets hold of men for his gang. He begins by offering a man a bribe for a small misdemeanour, for something not quite straight (for something which appears simple and perfectly safe). Then he goes on to offer more for something definitely crooked . . . and the wretched victim daren't say no. Finally when the victim is thoroughly in his power Spinner enlists him in his band of brigands. You say that the information he wanted was worthless, so it wouldn't have mattered whether you gave it to him or not, but it's quite possible that Spinner knew it was worthless and was just trying to tempt you to take the first step on the downward path.'

Gerald considered this thoughtfully. It might be true. If so it was diabolically clever! In his own mind he felt more than ever certain that the man who had beaten him up was the Spinner but he saw that there had to be proof. He said slowly: 'The man who questioned me and assaulted me was wearing big dark spectacles which hid his face, but you could identify him by his fingerprints, couldn't you? He wasn't wearing gloves.'

'That's just what we can't do,' replied Major Kane regretfully. 'The room is old and exceedingly dirty. There are dozens of fingerprints all over the place. It looks as if it hasn't been cleaned for years.'

'Probably it hasn't,' said Mac, nodding. 'Mrs Raddle is dirty and lazy.'

'There was one thing I noticed,' Gerald said. 'I was watching his hands when he was spreading out the map. His hands were unusual: they were small and white and the fingers were short and stubby . . . but I wouldn't like to identify him by that. It was a map of MacCallum's Ship-Yard. He had made it himself and was rather proud of it so he was furious when I tore it to bits and chucked it into the waste-paper basket . . . The map!' cried Gerald, sitting up in bed in his excitement. 'The map. Oh, what a fool I am! Why didn't I think of it before? He took it out of an envelope and spread it on the table . . . so of course it will have his fingerprints on it: his and mine!'

'You tore it up and dropped it into the waste-paper basket?'

'Yes.'

Major Kane didn't wait for more. He turned and ran out of the room and down the stairs. They heard him start his car and roar off up the road.

Gerald sighed and lay back on his pillow. 'It's too late,' he said wearily. 'Mrs Raddle has probably emptied the basket and burned the contents.'

'Unlikely,' Mac declared. 'Mrs Raddle is a lazy slut. Of course if it had been Kirsty she would have tidied up the room thoroughly.'

There was a short silence.

'How is everybody?' asked Gerald at last.

'Everybody is fine,' replied Mac cheerfully. 'You will be sorry to hear that our dear friend Oliver took the huff at something I said and left us. He has gone to stay with Lucius Cottar, of course.'

'Of course,' agreed Gerald.

'Kirsty is in particularly good form. She was humming the MacGregors' Lament this morning – a sure sign that she's happy – Malcolm is happy too. He said to me that it was a pity Mister Stoddart did not kill the Royal – but he didn't mean it.'

'Poor Stoddart!' said Gerald smiling. 'He isn't popular, is he?'

Mac hesitated and then said, 'Gerald, listen! I've got to go to London next week. I don't want to go – I'm a country cousin – but Major Kane wants me. I saw two of those men in MacTaggart's Public Bar and had a good look at them so I would know them again. All I shall have to do is to pick them out from a crowd of other men. See?'

Gerald nodded. He wondered what was coming.

'Then there's Donny,' continued Mac. 'Donny's father has

written to say she's to come home. If she comes with me I can drop her at Larchester: it's on my way so it wouldn't be any bother and it would save her the expense of her railway fare. (They're rather badly off, you know.) Last, but not least, I can pick up a friend on the way back. He's a captain in the gunners and a good shot with a rifle so he can help me to cull the hinds.'

'You've got it all worked out,' suggested Gerald.

'Yes, it fits in quite well . . . but it means that Phil will be alone at Tigh na Feidh. I don't like the idea at all. I wondered if you could come back and stay with her until—'

'I can't!' interrupted Gerald. 'I've had my holiday. I must go back to Glasgow and do some work.'

'You aren't fit—'

'I'll soon be better. Dr Wedderburn says I can drive back if I stay a night on the way.'

'Oh, I say! Couldn't you stay for a week? You won't be fit for stalking but a quiet lazy time at Tigh na Feidh is just what you need. I'd feel much happier if you were there with Phil.'

'Malcolm and Kirsty will be there, won't they?'

'Yes, of course – and they're very good value in their own line – but they aren't very bright if anything unexpected happens.'

'What could happen?'

'Oh, I don't know,' replied Mac, frowning. 'Major Kane thinks he's got all those devils safely under lock and key but they're as slippery as eels, aren't they?'

Gerald couldn't deny this. He remembered what the Spinner had said about bolts and bars and guard-dogs.

'Do stay,' urged Mac. 'Sir Walter wouldn't mind, I'm sure.'

No, thought Gerald, Walter wouldn't mind. Walter would be only too willing to extend his holiday. It was Gerald himself who 'minded'. He had decided that he must banish

Phil from his heart (it would be terribly difficult of course
but she was not for him and the sooner he got over his
madness the better). A week in her company at Tigh na
Feidh wouldn't help his love-lorn condition.

'Do say you will,' pleaded Mac. 'You're so dependable,
Gerald. I know you're fed up with Phil but—'

'Fed up with Phil?' Gerald exclaimed. 'Good heavens.
No! Phil is marvellous! There's nobody like her in the
Whole Wide World! I'm mad about her! I shall always
love her as long as I live; but she doesn't love me. She
made that perfectly clear. So I've just got to bear it. I've got
to get over it as best I can . . . but I don't know how I
can ever get over it,' added Gerald hopelessly.

'It's queer,' said Mac, looking at his friend in surprise.

'What's queer,' asked Gerald.

'I mean this "love-business" seems a bit dotty. Oh well, it
can't be helped.'

Mac turned to go but Gerald called him back. 'I'll do
it,' said Gerald. 'I'll go back to Tigh na Feidh and stay for
a week – if Phil wants me.'

'Oh, it was Phil's idea,' said Mac.

He was whistling cheerfully as he ran downstairs : Mac
was always happy when he had got exactly what he wanted.

Gerald was tired now and his head was aching so he
snuggled down in bed and shut his eyes. He was almost
asleep when a slight movement aroused him. He opened his
eyes and found himself looking into a small face covered with
brown freckles and topped by a bush of bright red hair. The
owner of the bush was kneeling beside the bed so the face
was very close – and the blue eyes which were gazing at
him wore a somewhat anxious expression.

'Hullo, Sandy!' said Gerald sleepily.

'I did not waken you, Mister Gerald. Mother said I was

not to waken you. I was just waiting for you to waken by yourself. I was as quiet as quiet.'

Gerald wasn't sure whether or not Sandy had wakened him but he said soothingly, 'I wasn't really asleep. What's the matter, Sandy?'

'I was wanting to ask you something,' Sandy explained. 'It was on Wednesday. I was searching for you, and at last I saw you on the hill. I was meaning to speak to you when those men came along. They were shouting at you – and swearing at you – and the fat one had a rifle . . .'

'I know.'

'I was frightened he would shoot you – and then I saw you had the legs of them so I hid in the heather till they passed and then I stalked them. It was easy stalking them – they never looked behind – they were watching you all the time.'

Gerald was interested in this recital. 'What next?' he inquired.

'You led them into the bog so I left them there and ran after you. I was wanting to ask you something. I followed you through the pine woods and down to the river and I saw you climbing the big tree. I thought you had jinked them so I waited a bit. I was just going to call to you – I was wanting to ask you something – when I heard them coming. They sat down beneath the tree. The fat one was panting. His face was very red.'

'Did you hear them talking, Sandy?'

Sandy nodded. 'It was funny sort of talk, Mister Gerald. I could not be understanding what they said – except about Raddles' Inn. Then away they went, up the river to find you! I was laughing to myself about it—'

'They came back and caught me in a sack like a rabbit,' said Gerald bitterly.

'They were bad men,' declared Sandy. 'They put the sack over your head and threw you on the ground and kicked you. Then they carried you away. If I had a little rifle, like Miss Phil, I could have shot them – and I would, too.'

'What did you do?' asked Gerald.

'I waited for a wee while. Then I waded across the river and ran to Uncle Jamie and I told him. He was in a great way. He telephoned to Major Kane and he put out the signal for the Fire Brigade to come . . . and off they went in Uncle Jamie's car. There was six of them and there was no room for me so I went home.'

This seemed to be the end of the story. 'It was the right thing to do,' Gerald told him. 'You couldn't have done anything better. Was that what you wanted to ask me?'

'It was not,' replied Sandy promptly. 'I was wanting to ask you about lions. Lions are brave. When lions are wounded they attack you – and kill you – and eat you. I was wondering about bools. Bools are not wanting to eat you. Bools eat grass – like stags – but they attack you just the same. Why do they, Mister Gerald?'

Gerald was tired now. His headache was getting worse (it was like a steam-hammer thumping in his head) but he owed this child so much that he felt obliged to answer the questions. I owe him my life, thought Gerald, looking at the freckled face, so near his own, with affection. (It occurred to Gerald quite suddenly that it would be very pleasant to have a little son of eleven years old. Not quite like Sandy, of course, because his own little son would have dark hair and hazel eyes . . . but that was madness!)

'Why do they, Mister Gerald?'

'Bulls are bad-tempered,' suggested Gerald feebly.

Obviously this answer was not entirely satisfactory. 'Why are they bad-tempered?' Sandy inquired.

'I don't know.'

Sandy continued, 'There was a bool attacked Mister Ross but Mister Mackenzie took a pitchfork and went for it and drove it away. I would take a pitchfork and go for a bool that was attacking you, Mister Gerald.'

'That would be very kind of you.'

'But there were two big men,' said Sandy regretfully.

For a moment Gerald was puzzled . . . then he saw the point.

'It wouldn't have been any good,' he said firmly. 'You did the right thing, Sandy. You did the sensible thing: you used your head.'

'I was frightened,' admitted Sandy with a sigh.

Gerald sighed too: the pain in his head was almost unbearable.

'Is your head sore?' asked Sandy sympathetically.

'Yes.'

'Will it be better tomorrow?'

'I hope so.'

'Could you tell me one more thing?'

'Tomorrow, Sandy.'

'Just one more,' said Sandy in wheedling tones.

'What is it?'

'Which is the bravest: bools or lions?'

This was much too difficult for Gerald in his present condition. He groaned feebly and shut his eyes.

'Are you wanting to sleep, Mister Gerald?' enquired his tormentor.

'Yes.'

'Will you be telling me tomorrow?'

'Yes.'

There was a slight sound. The door opened . . . then shut very quietly. Sandy had gone.

Peace – heavenly peace – descended upon the bare little room and Gerald slept.

26 Which tells how Phil carried out her idea

It had been Phil's idea that Gerald should come to Tigh na Feidh for a week's convalescence. She wanted to look after him and coddle him until he had recovered from his horrible experience. She had decided to give him breakfast in bed, to feed him well and to keep him warm and cheerful.

The weather had worsened. There was frost at night and the wind was from the north. The rut had begun: the stags came down from the hill-tops and roared in the early morning. There was ice on the Perilous Road.

Phil had never lived at Tigh na Feidh so late in the year but the alterations at the Big House were not yet completed so she stayed on with Malcolm and Kirsty and was comfortable enough . . . but now she began to look about her and to wonder whether it would be comfortable for an invalid. She consulted Kirsty and Kirsty entered into the spirit of the thing. She liked Mister Gerald. It was Kirsty who said that the Tower Room was cold and damp and suggested that the South bedroom (which was over the kitchen) would be warmer.

Malcolm agreed and pointed out that the South bedroom had the advantage of a chimney which didn't smoke (all the other bedroom chimneys were full of jackdaws' nests and had been completely blocked ever since Malcolm could remember).

He put a new cord in the window and oiled the lock of the door (these were jobs he had intended to perform for weeks). Then he brought several loads of wood and piled them beside the fire-place. Meantime Kirsty had given the room a thorough turn out.

Phil took the Land-Rover and went down to the village . . . and the first person she saw, coming out of the post office, was Dr Wedderburn. She stopped to speak to him, to explain her idea and to ask his advice.

'That's good news,' declared the doctor. 'Oh yes, I know I said he could go back to Glasgow but a week or ten days at Tigh na Feidh will be very much better. His cuts and bruises have healed – he's a healthy young man – but the treatment he received has been a shock to his nervous system. Don't coddle him of course but keep him warm and cosy.'

'Yes, of course,' agreed Phil. 'What about food, Doctor?'

'Milk and eggs; fresh fruit and vegetables; chops and steaks, porridge and cream and wholemeal bread,' replied Doctor Wedderburn. 'A glass of burgundy would do him no harm. I've given him a sedative to help him to sleep – and a cup of warm milk at bedtime would be just the thing to send him off to dreamland.' The doctor's eyes twinkled and he added, 'If he gets bored, talking to you, Malcolm can teach him to tie flies and he can read Jane Austen. Goodbye, Phil.'

'Goodbye, Doctor,' said Phil breathlessly.

She watched him drive off down the road – he was always in a hurry – but it didn't matter: she had got what she wanted.

Her next port of call was the Big House. Here she found a hearth-rug, an eiderdown quilt, a pair of red rep curtains and a bed table so she packed these invalid comforts into the Land-Rover.

The doctor had said his patient was to read Jane Austen. Phil approved of this: Jane was soothing. So Phil went into the library and looked at the shelf of Miss Austen's books. *Persuasion* was her own favourite; she was sure Gerald would like it . . . but then she remembered that

Louisa had fallen down the steps at Lyme Regis and had injured her head, so perhaps it wasn't a good choice? Phil considered the matter and then took *Northanger Abbey*: Gerald had a sense of humour so Catherine's behaviour would amuse him.

Finally she took an electric torch and went down the stone steps to the cellar. Here she discovered ten bottles of burgundy. A dozen had been given to MacAslan by Sir Walter MacCallum as a Christmas present and it was produced only on Special Occasions. Phil herself didn't appreciate it, but obviously it must be 'good'. After a few moments' hesitation she took two bottles, put them into a wine-basket and carried them carefully upstairs. She had been well-trained. It was a pity she had to take them to Tigh na Feidh over the Perilous Road, but she must just drive slowly and as smoothly as possible so as not to upset her delicate passengers.

On the way home Phil called on Mr MacTaggart and asked him to ring up the butcher at Kincraig and order chops and steaks and a piece of hough for broth. MacTaggart replied that he would be delighted to do so . . . and made several sensible suggestions: he produced two dozen eggs and a basket of fruit and offered to send the daily paper and the letters and three pints of milk to Tigh na Feidh every morning. It would be no trouble at all: the lad could take them. The lad was eating his head off and the walk would do him good. If there was anything else that Miss Phil wanted she had only to make a list and give it to the lad. Mr MacTaggart would see to it himself.

Having settled all this in a satisfactory manner Phil sat down in the MacTaggarts' private parlour for a cup of tea and a cosy chat. As usual Mr MacTaggart was full of information and only too willing to pass it on: four plain-clothes detectives had come from London and had made a thorough search of The Horseman's Inn.

'It was the chief of the gang that was killed?' suggested Phil.

'That is so,' agreed Mr MacTaggart, smiling cheerfully. 'They call him the Spinner for he was the one that planned all the raids and the robberies . . . and Major Kane is pleased about that for he kept himself in the background so maybe it would have been difficult to be proving anything against him. There were three shots – I heard them myself – and the policemen from London found the weapon that had fired the bullets but there is no telling who it belonged to. It had been wiped clean and kicked under the table. You see, Miss Phil, there is some way of knowing which pistol has fired the bullets – and all the bullets had been fired out of the same weapon. The sergeant from Kincraig was showing me the funny wee pistol. It was not like the Ardfalloch lads' pistols that they had over from the war . . . but maybe I should not be telling you that,' added Mr MacTaggart doubtfully.

Phil assured him that she wouldn't mention it to anybody. As a matter of fact she had heard most of it from Mac, but some of it was News. Having listened with interest to Mr MacTaggart's story Phil was quite prepared to tell him about Mac's trip to London . . . but there was nothing she could tell him that he didn't know already. He knew that Mac had left Ardfalloch the day before yesterday, was breaking his journey at Larchester and then going on to London to meet Major Kane . . . and Mrs MacTaggart had heard at a meeting of the Women's Rural Institute that 'Mister Stoddart' had left Tigh na Feidh and had gone to stay with a friend at Ascot.

How did they know 'all that', wondered Phil, as she drove home slowly and carefully up the Perilous Road. It didn't matter of course because she had nothing to hide but all the same it was a mystery and even the 'peep-hole' into the Public Bar could not account for it.

27 Tells how Mac solved all the problems

Gerald had been reluctant to return to Tigh na Feidh: he had feared that his relationship with Phil might be awkward; but Phil had told him that she wanted him as her friend and it was as a friend that she received him. This was all the easier because she was his hostess and had inherited the true Highland tradition of hospitality to a guest. Last, but by no means least, Phil's guest was pale, beneath his suntan, and the scar on his eyebrow was still visible: it was obvious that he had had a bad time and required care.

Gerald had no idea of the elaborate arrangements which had been made for his benefit but he *did* realise that he was extremely comfortable: the fire in his bedroom was a luxury he enjoyed. He still felt tired and lazy and a little giddy at times so it was pleasant to be cosseted by Phil and Kirsty. Malcolm, also, was unusually kind . . . there was a conspiracy of kindness which created a very peaceful pleasant atmosphere in the house.

Doctor Wedderburn had said that the patient was not to be 'coddled' so one fine morning Phil took him for a short walk. She took her .22 rifle, intending to shoot a fox which had been marauding Malcolm's hen-run but her mind was not on the job so wily old reynard eluded his huntress without difficulty.

The afternoons were cold and unpleasant so Phil drew the curtains and she and Gerald had tea together beside the dining-room fire: it was extremely cosy. Sometimes they chatted and learnt a great deal about each other – they had had no opportunity of intimate talk before – and sometimes they sat together in silent companionship: Phil with her knitting and Gerald watching her flying fingers or reading *Northanger Abbey* and chuckling. (Gerald was an ardent admirer of Miss Austen and *Northanger Abbey* was the only one of her books which he had not read.)

Gerald was still desperately in love with Phil and now that he was beginning to know her better, he found himself loving her more tenderly than before and appreciating her goodness and kindness and unselfishness! A very sweet companionship grew up between them.

It was on the third day, when Mr MacTaggart's lad had come with the milk and the mail (and was having tea in the kitchen with Kirsty) that Phil looked up from her letters and said: 'There isn't one from Mac! You haven't got one either, have you, Gerald? He said he would write when he got to London. What can he be doing?'

'He may have changed his plans,' suggested Gerald. 'Mac isn't a great letter-writer, is he? I expect he's waiting till he gets home to tell us all the news.'

'He will be in London now,' said Phil frowning.

Gerald agreed that he would be in London. It was strange to think of Mac in London. Mac was so much a part of Ardfalloch that it was difficult to imagine him elsewhere . . . especially difficult to imagine him amongst the crowds and the traffic and the noise of a big city! Mac would be as out of place, walking down Piccadilly, as a Royal Stag.

But nobody will know, thought Gerald smiling to himself. Not one of the busy throng, rubbing shoulders with Mac, will realise that he is rubbing shoulders with a wild Highlander from the North. Mac, in his town clothes, looks just like other young men except that he is unusually good-looking.

Gerald explained this idea to Phil and discovered that she understood – and was interested – but did not agree. 'I think I would know,' she said thoughtfully.

'You would be too busy to notice,' Gerald told her. 'You would be too taken up with your own affairs to notice a stag. You would be thinking about stocks and shares, bulls and bears, or hastening to a directors' meeting, or—'

'Oh Gerald, you *are* silly,' said Phil, laughing.

Gerald laughed too. He knew he was silly but he had made Phil laugh and forget (for the moment) her anxiety about her brother.

Doctor Wedderburn had said 'early to bed', and Phil was carrying out his orders to the letter, so at ten o'clock she rose and suggested that they should 'make it a day'.

Gerald had snibbed the windows and Phil was putting the guard on the fire when the door opened and Mac walked in.

'Mac!' exclaimed Phil and Gerald in amazement.

'Yes, it's me,' agreed Mac, grinning.

'What has happened?' asked Phil in alarm.

'Nothing,' replied Mac. 'I mean an awful lot has happened. Oh, I know you weren't expecting me but I had to come. I never went near London. I just came in a hurry because I wanted to see you and explain. Donny said "ask Phil, she'll know what to do about it".'

'About what?'

'About Donny's father. He'll be furious, of course. The point is: should we tell him or not?'

Gerald was waiting patiently for the point to be arrived at but Phil was not so patient.

'Why will he be furious? What have you done? Tell us about it for goodness' sake!' she exclaimed.

'All right, keep your hair on,' suggested her brother. 'I'm telling you about it. I could tell you better if you didn't keep on interrupting me—'

'I'm not interrupting you—'

'Yes, you are. I've come all this way, driving like Jehu, to tell you that you can get married whenever you like. There's nothing to prevent you. See?'

'Mac, what on earth are you talking about?'

'About you and Gerald.'

'You're crazy,' Phil declared. 'Who's going to look after Ardfalloch? Who's going to look after Daddy? Who's going to—'

'Donny and I, of course. We're going to be married.'

'You're going to be married?' asked Phil incredulously.

'Why not? Dad is very fond of Donny – and Donny thinks the world of "MacAslan" – so that's all right. And Donny likes Ardfalloch. You know that, don't you? She thinks Ardfalloch is "just like heaven". You've heard her say it, haven't you?'

'But what about you?'

'What about me?' asked Mac in surprise.

'Do you love Donny?'

'Yes, of course!'

'You never said . . .'

'Oh, I know!' agreed Mac, sitting down and holding his head in his hands. 'I know it sounds crazy but it isn't, really. When Donny was here, two years ago, I liked her. I thought she was nice and she liked me. There was no silly nonsense about it: we just liked each other. This year I liked her even better. I thought she was sweet. She *is* sweet. She's sweet and kind and – and gentle. She's amusing, too, in her own quiet way. Then I took her home to Larchester and stayed there for a couple of days (you know that, of course)! It was when I was there that I realised the truth: it was when I heard that foul old man being rude and sarcastic and saw Donny curling up like a sea-anemone! IT MADE ME SEE RED,' declared Mac, seizing tufts of his hair as if he intended to pull it out by the roots. 'I was so furious that I could have killed him. I wanted to kill him. I wanted to put my hands round his throat and strangle him. It was quite frightening, you know. I've never felt like that before.'

Mac paused for a few moments: his hearers gazed at him in alarm.

Then he continued: 'I wanted to strangle him – but I couldn't of course. I mean I could have strangled him quite easily (his throat is thin and stringy, like a chicken) but he's Donny's father and he's old and frail. He's older than Dad with a bald head and a scrubby grey beard . . . and he's clever. He's much too clever for me. As a matter of fact he was quite polite to me in a nasty sort of way but he knows exactly how to make Donny squirm.'

'Squirm!' echoed Phil in horrified tones.

'Yes. I had to sit there and watch her turning pale and squirming. She's terrified of him. Oh, he doesn't beat her with sticks; he just beats her with words.'

'You're sorry for her—'

'No, I'm not! At least I am, of course, but it isn't because I'm sorry for her that I'm going to marry her. It's because I discovered that I love her – frightfully. It's because I want to – to pick her up in my arms and bring her home to Ardfalloch and make her happy for ever and ever.'

There was silence.

'Don't you understand?' asked Mac impatiently.

Of course they understood.

Gerald understood because he felt exactly the same about Phil: he loved her – frightfully. He wanted to pick her up in his arms and take her home and make her happy for ever and ever. Phil understood because she knew Mac: she knew him inside out.

'Mac,' said Phil, very seriously, 'Does Donny love you?'

'Yes, she does!' replied Mac triumphantly. 'It's amazing, isn't it? Donny loves me. It makes me feel seven feet tall and as strong as an ox. It makes me feel like a stag with fourteen points. Donny loves me and she's going to marry me.'

'What will her father do without her?'

'That's the snag,' agreed Mac. 'That's what I came to see you about. Should we tell him or not? He'll kick up a dust, of course – that goes without saying. Donny keeps house for him; she cooks and cleans and washes and mends his clothes. She's just an unpaid drudge – so naturally he won't want to lose her services. Nobody else would do all that – and do it for nothing. Nobody else would stand his beastly rudeness . . . but it doesn't matter.'

'Doesn't matter?'

'Not a hoot,' said Mac cheerfully. 'If the horrid old man objects we shall just have to wait until she's twenty-one – and she's going to be twenty-one next month. After that she's free to do what she wants and she wants to marry me. See what I mean?'

They saw.

'So you can go ahead and get married as soon as you like.'

'But, Mac—'

'Dad will be all right,' interrupted Mac. 'Donny and I will live with him at Ardfalloch of course. We'll look after him and keep him happy . . . and you can come up from Glasgow and stay with us as often as you want. That's right, isn't it, Gerald?'

'Yes, of course!'

'But Mac—' began Phil.

'Don't keep on saying BUT,' said Mac, somewhat unreasonably. 'I've come here to solve all our problems (Major Kane will be annoyed with me if I'm not in London to meet him at the appointed time). I've come here at great inconvenience – and all you say is BUT! What are you butting about, Phil?'

'About Simon,' replied Phil in a very small voice.

'Simon!' said Mac scornfully. 'Goodness gracious, Phil! You're not worrying about Simon, are you? Simon doesn't love you – not like I love Donny. If Simon loved you – like I love Donny – he wouldn't be content to let things drift. He would want to marry you straight off – like I want to marry

Donny. And what's more,' said Mac firmly. 'What's more if you loved Simon – like Donny loves me – you wouldn't be content to drift either. I didn't realise this before, of course. It's only now that I see it clearly, it's only now that I understand.'

'He's right, you know,' said Gerald.

Of course he was right. Phil had seen already that Mac knew what he was talking about.

She said feebly, 'But it seems unkind—'

'It would be unkind to marry Simon if you don't love him,' declared Mac. 'Of course if you want to be Lady Wentworth and live at Limbourne—'

'I don't!'

'Well then, don't. Don't swither, Phil. Make up your mind: here's Gerald, who loves you madly and wants to marry you straight off . . . and there's Simon who's having a rattling good time at Cambridge, dancing and playing cricket and speechifying at the Debating Society or whatever it's called . . .'

Gerald was listening to all this. He had thought of inter-vening and then he had realised that it would be a mistake: Mac was fighting his battle for him and was making a much better job of it than he could have done. It was because Mac knew Phil so well. It was because he was her brother: they had grown up together; they had shared things; they had been in scrapes together; they had quarrelled and made it up and had become better friends than ever. For a moment Gerald felt a twinge of jealousy (however long he knew Phil, however dearly he loved her, he would never be able to understand her – like this) and then he smiled at his own folly. It's like Bess and me, thought Gerald. Walter worships the ground Bess treads on but he will never be able to understand her as I do because he didn't know her as a child.

'You needn't marry either of them,' Mac was saying. 'You

can marry Oliver if you like. He told me he had asked
you and—'

'I wouldn't marry Oliver if he were the only man in the
world!'

Mac nodded seriously. 'I think you're right. If I had to
live with Oliver he would drive me mad in a week.'

'He would drive me mad in three days,' Phil declared
with mounting fury.

'Or you needn't marry any of them,' Mac continued.
'You can stay at Ardfalloch. Donny and I will be delighted
– so will Dad. We all love you dearly: you know that, don't
you?'

'How silly you are!' cried Phil. 'Of course I want to marry
Gerald. I love him just as much as you love Donny – probably more! All I want to know is: what am I to do about
Simon? How am I to tell him? He has never asked me to
marry him: it has just been an understood thing. How can
you write and say you don't want to marry someone when he
hasn't asked you?'

'You can write and say you're going to marry Gerald.
That's the best way. That's the honest way, Phil.'

Phil's eyes were bright with tears. She turned to Gerald
and held out her hands. 'Oh Gerald, what am I to do?'

Gerald hesitated.

'Go on, kiss her!' hissed Mac – and fled. He paused at
the door for a moment and saw that his advice was being
taken with enthusiasm.